TWICE TOLD TALES

OTHER BOOKS BY DANIEL STERN

The Girl with the Glass Heart

The Guests of Fame

Miss America

Who Shall Live, Who Shall Die

After the War

The Suicide Academy

The Rose Rabbi

Final Cut

An Urban Affair

TWICE TOLD TALES

stories

By Daniel Stern

PARIS
REVIEW
EDITIONS

The Liberal Imagination by Lionel Trilling: a story, was first published in the magazine New Letters.

The Interpretation of Dreams by Sigmund Freud: a story, was first published in The Ontario Review and was included in O'Henry Prize Stories: 1987, The Best American Short Stories: 1987 and The Ways We Live Now: Contemporary Short Fiction From The Ontario Review.

Brooksmith by Henry James: a story, was first published in the magazine Raritan.

The Psychopathology of Everyday Life by Sigmund Freud: a story, was first published in the Paris Review.

Copyright 1989 by Daniel Stern
All rights reserved
including the right of reproduction
in whole or in part in any form
Published by Paris Review Editions/British American Publishing
3 Cornell Road
Latham, NY 12110
Manufactured in the United States of America

93   92   91   90   89   5   4   3   2   1

Library of Congress Cataloging-in-Publication Data

Stern, Daniel, 1928—
Twice told tales.

I. Title.
PS3569.T3887T88   1989   813'.54   88-35199
ISBN 0-945167-13-X

This book is for Melissa, Joshua, Beverly and Eric.

And it goes to them with love.

CONTENTS

There is a kind of stimulus for a writer which is more important than the stimulus of admiring another writer. . . . This relation is a feeling of profound kinship, or rather of a peculiar personal intimacy, with another, probably a dead author . . . it is something more than encouragement to you. It is a cause of development, like personal relations in life. Like personal intimacies in life, it may and probably will pass, but it will be ineffaceable.

T.S. ELIOT

THE LIBERAL
IMAGINATION
BY LIONEL TRILLING

a story

Does anyone here know the precise meaning of the word *eulogy*? Come on: you're all word people.

Does any one of you know the exact meaning of the word *liberal*? No, for God's sake, don't raise your hands. This isn't a classroom. Don't you have a sense of the fitness of things? Look at you: editors, novelists, publishers, poets, publicity people (I see at least one concert pianist and one cellist), advertising executives, professors. And you don't know any better?

It occurs to me, as I look around at this group, that you can be divided into two groups: the central and the peripheral. And I wonder how you see—or saw—poor Katherine Eudemie—her one novel, fourteen poems, six book reviews, and several hundred grant applications. Don't get restless or nervous. I won't be any worse than the conventional choice for this situation; a minister or rabbi. I name two since Katherine was born Protestant but so many of you are Jewish—and she loved you for your Jewishness. Came to New York seeking it, your Jewishness, her fortune; they seemed somehow intertwined. Well, I have been attacked, challenged, provoked, as the "shadow-Jew" of Katherine's early years, by her husband Jackson—all to convince me to speak at the funeral of his wife. The question is: Does Jackson Eudemie know that on a magnificent spring night, years, yes decades ago, I desecrated his beloved wife, Katherine? Of course she wasn't his beloved wife yet. In fact it was on that night that they first met: at the home of Lionel Trilling, author of *The Liberal Imagination*, a party after which took place the shameful incident of the blindfold, the desecration of Katherine

3

Eudemie. She was drunk on gin—this was before vodka—and submitted to me under strange circumstances.

Desecration: to remove from anything its sacred character. To profane or unhallow.

You understand these definitions, these hints and apostrophes with which I delay all the excitement to come: midnight sexual encounters, blindfolds, comic turns, a baby forgotten in the cloakroom of a midtown restaurant, high moments of intellectual adventure with some of the most brilliant of the time—these interruptions are a hazard of my occupation.

I am a copyeditor, freelance. Interrupting is my job, digression is my mother tongue. I explicate terms the way other people chew food. And I'm proud of one fact: when I tackle the work of an author—there is no forest, only trees! I'm also proud of my identity. I am the only life-long, freelance copyeditor in the United States. If at the top of the literary ladder stands the Nobel laureate novelist or poet, who can stand on the bottom rung? No—I do even better. I *am* the bottom rung! And it is my great pleasure to be the lowest rung on the ladder. What joy. Not nowhere to go but up. I lost *that* illusion years ago. No. *Nowhere to go!* It's hard to communicate to my contemporaries the peculiar pleasures of starting in a cul-de-sac—so that you can't possibly come to one.

Ah, some of you are now thinking here's where he tells us he's really a writer. This freelance copyediting dodge is just a cover. Wrong! I have only one story to tell and that's why I'm here today. For this is my story of how I desecrated Katherine Eudemie on one of the most balmy, exquisitely forgiving spring nights so many thousands of nights ago; a night that changed my life.

Let me present to you this sturdy wheat-colored girl.

Wheat-colored?

Yes.

The girl, herself?

Yes. I would have marked cl. for cliché in the margin for wheat-colored hair, say. But all of Katherine Eudemie evoked shades of wheat. I knew. I'd seen wheatfields in movies when I was a kid. Later, on the train to Fort Ord, Indiana, en route to basic training during the Korean unpleasantness which followed the "recent" unpleasantness and preceded the Vietnam unpleasantness, I'd seen wheatfields blurring by from the train window.

And I am correct. As Katherine undressed that night, post-party, pre-desecration, in the half-darkness of that tiny Village apartment, her body was definitely wheat-colored from long legs to crown. A kind of amber-light-brownish, with tints of yellow fading in and out. I hope you understand that there is the chaos of memory and the distance of time to deal with. And, since I do not share the graphomania of my generation and have only this one story to tell, I'm trying to be as true as I can to the details. Someone has said God rests in the detail. And as I recall for myself and you that party at the Trillings, and this young woman fresh out of Oak Park, Illinois, by way of the University of Chicago, this one detail presents itself with authority: the wheat-like coloring of that long-limbed lovely body now prematurely harvested. I know, I know, they're all premature. But she was only forty something. That's pretty premature given the life insurance statistics, given her part-Cherokee Indian blood (her claim, unsubstantiated), given the fact that she began as a gifted poet of ferocious ambition, wrote one published novel at twenty-three, appropriately titled The Country of the Young, one produced play, and followed those by hundreds of grants and summers at Yaddo and MacDowell. Not one line of print by or about her ever appeared again.

Given all that. All after having been desecrated by

me on a night of moonlit clouds, of pure calligraphic
wonder.

Who's that talking to Trilling?"
"Steve Marcus. He invented Victorian pornography."
"Then why are they talking about fishing? Dry flies,
wet flies. The moment of my intellectual life and they're
talking trout. Where's Jane Austen? Where's E. M. Forster?"
"You're sure it's fishing? Maybe it's sex. Dry flies,
wet flies . . ." She liked to play at being lewder-than-
thou.

I knew why she'd taken me to Lionel Trilling's home.
Because I was not only a literaphile (there's no such
word: it's my neologism for someone who loves liter-
ature, not merely books, as in bibliophile) but I was
also an autodidact. She knew I'd be doubly delighted
by the quality of the discourse: Bloomsbury on Morningside Heights.
There was no way for her to know I would tease a
stony-faced Huntress of Ideas:
"Where did you go to school?"
"I'm an autodidact."
"Really?"
"Yes. I taught myself to drive."
Beware! Those who tease the gods will be punished.
In the first case by talk of fish instead of Forster. But
after fish (and much wine) came dessert. Katherine
Eudemie. We'd been engaged in the usual sexual spar-
ring (it's no accident that in sparring the fighters are
called partners. A fight is only a fight. Sparring is a

relationship). And our relationship, about forty hours old, was bouncing along its competitive, sexy way; myself, Jewish, New Yorkish, bookish, twenty-fiveish. Katherine Eudemie, gentile, Judaphile, turning twenty-five in a short while.

She was my first encounter with the stream of wheatcolored young women traveling West to East in search of their promised Jews; the Rose Rabbis of their flowering literary, political, and sexual ambitions. The dark strangers between whose temples, arms, and legs wisdom was to be found, and whose wisdom was aphrodisiac.

I had no wisdom to offer. I had then what I have now: a rag-bag of quotations: the currency of the uneducated. It sufficed. A line from a Pound canto for an open-mouthed kiss. A Goethe aphorism for one brastrap down. A murmured memento from the Talmud to spread knees ever so slightly. Pretty good for forty hours of acquaintance this many years ago. I'm not being cruel. Cruelty requires a victim and an executioner. We were both victims. It was as thrilling to me as it was to Katherine. She came to me from Illinois that spring, singing songs of famous Chicago Jewish writers who refused to come East. Her affair with the most famous of them left a spoor on her skin. We both sniffed it to track each other around the bed.

Hence: sparring. Ducking, weaving, touching, panting, we were teaching each other the game in a match no one could win. Though, it turned out, *someone* could lose. My situation at the precise party-moment was the obverse of Katherine's. She had left her family to come East, raging to be known. *My* family had left *me* two months before I met Katherine Eudemie; left me for California. My quotations from de Tocqueville about restless, rootless Americans had been useless.

"There was no California, then," my father said, with

his optimism typically masquerading as logic. It was no help for me to point out that there was no California now either. Like Katherine he was enormously ambitious but it was not a vague, boundless ambition. It was precise and could be satisfied—by a great deal of money. Every enterprise failed him or vice-versa—it was never clear which was the case. He landed the first Volkswagen dealership in America. The guy with the second one made money. He bought land in Florida years after the whole country knew there was no land in Florida to buy. My mother's bitter joke in Yiddish: "Your father, the alchemist in reverse. *Fun gelt er macht dreck.*" Somewhere in the sunshine of California shimmered more gold. Like all good alchemists he believed in the magic of wealth and that getting it was a reasonable even scientific matter. He had ideas, he had plans, he had methods, he had obsessions. What he never had was the *gelt*.

I lingered on, pleasantly post-adolescent, amid the *dreck* of his dreams, carefully avoiding dreams of my own. All ambition was tainted. I assumed this was a temporary reaction. I had a tender tolerance for my own failure to get started.

It was a lively time. A college degree, my conspicuous lack, had not yet achieved the status of a high school diploma. That is, you could still get a job without one. Before leaving for the Golden West my father had arranged for my Uncle Harry—the flip side of my father, a true Midas—to pull strings at Duell Sloane & Pearce, a small but classy publisher, and J. Walter Thompson, an epic advertising agency. At the same time, an editor at N.Y.U. Press had offered me a manuscript to copyedit, a book on the language of sexual relations. I toyed with them all; a kind of languorous, lingering, professional foreplay.

"Getting involved with you is activity enough," I told Katherine.

"You're crazy," she said.

"No, you are; the mad alien invader. You're going to eat New York."

"I'm not *that* hungry."

"That's because you haven't had your first real taste."

"Oh? The review in the *Times* . . . ?"

"True. A taste."

She regretted having confessed that her Chicago hotshot had helped her place her novel. We'd argued, sparred, clothing and ideas all in disarray: her half-slip, Dostoyevsky's abominable politics, my shirt and half-opened fly, and the life and death of The Novel. Next to the bed on which we'd done everything except *it*, her ancient Royal Portable trembled on a tiny wooden table. She pointed to it.

"That's what placed my book."

"Easy does it," I said. "It's only been published and reviewed. It takes years to *place* a book."

"Is that a quotation?" she asked. Suspicion clouded the blue fields of her eyes.

"No. Just a cheap irony of my own. But true, anyway."

"Is it so awful to want a place, *my* place?"

I was merciless the way one is when being kept above bed instead of in bed.

"Are you sure it's your place—or *a* place; *any* place?"

She pressed red lips to my neck and mumbled, "Don't sell me so short. I'm not here just to make out. I want to find out, too." She stood up, a tall blonde apparition of confusion, wisps of hair everywhere. She blew some from the corners of her wide mouth. "To find out," she repeated.

I decided to be stupid.

"Find out what?"

"Everything."

"Everything Jewish, you mean."

Without smiling she said, "That's everything."

I grabbed her back to the bed, rolling on top of me; a roiling of unharvested wheat.

"God, I give up! The only parts of you not full of goyish nonsense are *these*."

I attacked these with mouth and hands.

All full of life, given the confusion, given the lust and the teasing, given the youth and the resentments. And all long before I had carved out my unique position as the bottom rung—America's only life-long, freelance copyeditor; even longer before my surprise fame as a funeral eulogist—the Georgie Jessel of the small-fry literati—had reached and convinced Jackson Eudemie that no one but I would do for the obsequies of poor, premature Katherine. Talk about finding your place. We found our places. Or they found us.

"You're so beautiful," I said in a rare abdication of irony. "No cosmetics. How do you do it?"

"With mirrors," she said. And, indeed, there were mirrors everywhere in that tiny Village apartment whose address I never knew.

Typical of the time and the immigrant-bohemian-style, she was staying in an apartment which had been loaned to a professor friend and who, in turn, loaned it to her; if you can loan what does not belong to you. I would guess you would simply have to give it if it's not yours. In any case, she had it—with no phone. One of the loaners or the other had carefully turned it off. It seemed to be significant that she could never get the address straight. It was one of those weird tripartite meetings of Christopher Street and two others. She always—the three times I went there with her—told the cab driver to turn here, turn there, stop here, and, presto, we were there. Where, we had no idea. (Once I went down to get cigarettes, just around the corner, and almost could not find my way back.) But when we were inside the apartment there were mirrors; tall, wooden, burnished, dark antique, a bureau mirror, tortoise-shell hand mirrors on every surface.

Yet she didn't seem to care for them; not for makeup, not for fussing hair, not for anything. Except for the moment before we entered Trillings' apartment. But that's because on the way up I'd made her weep.

We'd been talking about poetry as we walked. It's hard to believe, writing from the embattled city of now, that we so obliviously let stars creep from behind clouds, let the half-moon lighten, let night and shadows form around us with perfect insouciance as we walked and talked the hundred blocks from the West Village to Riverside Drive and Morningside Heights. We felt safe from everyone except each other.

"Why attack my poems?"

"I'm not. They were beautiful."

"Were."

"Are. It's their simple lyrical liberalism that worries me."

"Simple?"

"You don't even know which insult to get angry at. The word to worry about in that sentence is 'liberalism.'" I can see now, hundreds of thousands of words later, the copyeditor being born.

"You prefer fascism?"

Remember, this was back when fascism referred mainly to the recent unpleasantness. She whirled on me, grabbed my shoulders and shook me, the way men shook women in old movies.

"Are you doing this because I didn't let you?"

I took her hands from my shoulders and twisted an

arm up behind her back. She was a broad-shouldered farmgirl, stronger than I was. I had to play tough.

"Ah," I said. "It wouldn't be nice, not liberal, to be a son-of-a-bitch about your poetry just because you're torturing me by holding off making the beast with two backs."

The image distracted her. "What's that?" she said.

"*Othello*. act 1, scene 3."

" 'You're hurting my arm."

"Your trouble is not your parts, whether to allow me entry or not. Your problem is your heart."

"What's wrong with my heart?"

"It's in the right place. *You can't be a serious writer if your heart's in the right place.* Look at Eliot, look at Lawrence . . ." We were outside the apartment now. She stared into the hall mirror.

"Look at *me*," she murmured, brushing at her wet cheeks, "do I look awful?"

Awful?

She looked to be a wonderful, blonde portion of bruised innocence; terrorized by my attack, eager for the encounter to come, but terrified, too. Her Chicago mentor had been the go-between, had started her off. Now waited the dark intellectuals of New York, formidable, desirable, equal parts threat and promise.

My memory of the occasion, the guests, the conversation, is all quite vague. Since my life changed irrevocably that night—an event I'm still sorting out here—it's entirely possible that I confused people who were actually present with writers I met, read, or copyedited years later; possible that I have confused bursts of impromptu eloquence with what has been written and published since.

A minor legend has been formed around those days and these people. A kind of post-Lost Generation Goy's Guide to Literature. (I borrow the term from Katherine.

She kept what she called her Goy's Guide to New York in which she would note this or that word . . . pronouncing it with the care of a Japanese trying out an English word or phrase.

"What does Chutz-pah mean?"

"Never mind. You have it."

And after someone complimented her: "What does Shayne-Punim mean?"

"A thing of beauty and a joy forever.")

She also noted names with equal care. A partial listing in Katherine's Goy Guide: Trilling, Delmore Schwartz, Isaac Rosenfeld, Mailer (early), Harold Rosenberg, Philip Rahv, Bellow (very early), Sigmund Freud, Leon Trotsky, and Karl Marx, who, unfortunately, could not be at the party, but whose presence was still felt.

The war had been fought, fascism had been defeated, and the question of utopia, of socialism, was on everybody's mind.

On these minds especially.

Some minds.

Someone has said, when the half-gods go the gods arrive. What's more likely: when the gods go the half-gods arrive. Still, Mount Olympus has many addresses. And if these were half-gods, they would do!

I was still young. Not as young as Katherine Eudemie, who had after all written a novel called The Country of the Young. But young enough to be most attentive. I knew I was surrounded by a few rough equivalents of Apollo, Hermes, and that gang. If any of you want to get demanding about this, at least I'm sure about Auden. He didn't say much but he was on the premises. Though neither he nor Dwight Macdonald could get into Katherine's Guide, being goys themselves.

I'd read Dwight Macdonald's magazine *Politics*. And I'm pretty sure he was pouring a Scotch next to me at the makeshift bar; a large bear of a man with a Vandyke beard similar to my father's. Like my father he talked about money; apparently one could not make a living writing book reviews.

Hold it! I'm remembering Jacques Barzun. Also Isaac Rosenfeld (who I think may have been dead by then) and Norman Mailer. Put Rosenfeld down as a possible but not a strong one.

I'm afraid the only certainties I retain are the words; about them I am positive!

"A list of the writers of our time shows that liberal-progressivism was a matter of contempt or indifference to every writer of large mind—Proust, Joyce, Lawrence, Eliot, Mann (early), Kafka, Yeats, Gide, Shaw—probably there is not a name to be associated with a love of liberal democracy or a hope for it . . ."

Dammit, I remember Trilling saying that or something very like it, but he *couldn't* have. In fact, it turns out to be an entry in one of the journals he'd been keeping for years. Yet what he said threw Katherine Eudemie into a state of crazed rebellion, starting with an alcoholic catatonia and ending with sexual frenzy. Around those words and that state developed much of the evening's excitement: with results as varied as one desecration and one eventual marriage to Jackson Eudemie. Yes, he was present that night. How could he not be?

If the statement, accurate to the occasion or not, strikes you as less than shocking these days, remember, it was only six years earlier that the worldwide executioners had stopped mass-producing victims. And imagine Katherine, a child-bride and child-widow, as I learned minutes later, drawn from the conservative Middle West to Liberal New York. Consider her confusion, carrying her wounded heart right where it belonged, full of compassion, justice, and hope, only to be told that her international grand passions, her Prousts, her Joyces, her Eliots, had other fish to fry.

She downed two glasses of wine immediately. When more upsetting words arrived she downed two more.

"Don't try to keep up with me," she warned. "Jews can't drink."

She entered a sort of catatonic trance, during which we met, in quick order, Lionel and Diana Trilling, Jackson Eudemie, Lionel Abel, William Barrett, Jackson Eudemie, Norman Mailer, and Jackson Eudemie. I began to notice that Mr. Eudemie was hanging around us. I guessed *I* was not the attraction.

"I'm Jackson Eudemie."

"So I gather."

"I'm an editor at Doubleday. What do you do?"

"She's a writer."

"Can't *she* speak?"

"Sometimes."

"I'll wait."

He was tall, knife-thin, and seemed calm compared to that roomful of desperate characters. I don't mean desperate in the usual psychological way. I'm sure you know the kind of people whose every sentence, even the joking ones, *especially* the joking ones, imply hidden high stakes.

"I've been thinking more and more how much all of us comfortably ignore the demonic; yet it's everywhere now." Well, that kind of thing only said better, of course. But everything important; everything having *reach!*

Jackson Eudemie, on the other hand, was a kind of early-California. Cool when cool was still personal idiosyncrasy; before it became a cultural style. (And before it became a corrupt noun.) I shook him long enough to talk with some concern to Katherine.

"What's up?"

"Nothing."

"You're hiding out. Vanished behind your eyes."

"Leave me alone. Everybody isn't Jewish. I'm trying to work up my *chutz-pah*. Besides I hate what Trilling said."

Then she told me swiftly and sotto voce about her husband dying in shellfire at Normandy. Katherine and her husband, a couple of Minnesota Farmer-Labor Party kids, protesting the war, pushing socialism. (Trotsky and Marx came to *their* party.) But the war gobbled them up and spat them out. Widowed and not yet twenty-two, Katherine fled to Chicago, where she wrote a novel about a couple of Minnesota Farmer-Labor Party kids who believed and got to be, respectively, dead and widowed, all in the name of liberal democracy. Wrote it, however, with all the terrific modernist tricks you could pick up by smart reading and hanging around certain circles at the University of Chicago. She'd never expected to have her personal tragedy go smash against the new life she and her first novel had made.

"Doug volunteered," she said. "He didn't wait to be drafted. He *wanted* to sign up."

"And Ezra Pound didn't. Is that what's throwing you for a loop?"

"Don't try to out-tough me. It's too easy."

"You're going to do fine with this crowd. You think talk is serious. On the other hand, you'll have to give me a few minutes to get used to the idea that you never told me you were a widow."

"You never asked."

I was floundering, trying to pull her out of her funk. For the next half-hour or so I swam amid the themes and variations being sung all around me: "Demands of the Zeitgeist . . . Delmore and failure . . . Freud and Kafka . . ."

Or it may have been Delmore and Freud and Kafka and failure—it doesn't really matter.

No superior smiles, please. Ideas have a life cycle—youth, middle age, old age—like people: and there's that wonderful moment before they become conventions or gossip, when they ring like bells in the air of the mind. This was one of those moments. There was nothing stale or chewed over in this stuff then. All fresh as the milk that still came daily in glass bottles. Thus, bear in mind: I'm not dismissing with irony. I'm trying to remember and report with as much innocence as I can muster.

Nobody mentioned the war, pleasantly or unpleasantly. Russia was spoken of twice—once with warmth, once with anger.

After her first descent into shock Katherine rallied. Wine was her adrenalin. The more she took, the more animated she became. Groups formed around her. Jackson Eudemie's patience paid off. Finally, it turned out, Katherine *could* indeed speak. Words, laughter, wit, everything poured out as often as wine. She was the quintessential Golden Goya. (Useless to tell her that she had been using the masculine form of the noun.) She, trying to enchant the local rabbis, and Jackson, fighting for his share. For me, I was thinking about the dark death hidden behind all the yellow hair and stubborn eagerness to succeed, behind all the left-of-center laughter.

I was dimly aware that Katherine was conquering. The more aware I became, the more I withdrew to my own glass. Finally, I peeled Jackson from her side and we left. On the way home—a reeling, hundred-block drunken ballet of reversed steps—we had it all out. It was impossible to know who was drunker, or who was more in trouble.

"People don't die for anything, you know. They just die."

"A lie."

"Then you like human sacrifice?"

"I used to respect sacrifice."

"I haven't noticed."

"What does that mean?"

"You seem to be here to get, not to give up."

"I'm here to give and get."

"When does the giving start?"

"Don't mix up art with sex."

"No chance of confusion with you."

She broke our alcoholic lock-step to kiss me. In the midst of all the scents of a May night on New York streets—exhaust fumes mixed with soft spring air, distant cooking odors—I smelled berries.

"There," she said after the longest kiss we'd had yet, "just to introduce some confusion."

"What's that taste? What were you drinking?"

"Gin."

"Ah. Juniper berries. I thought you smelled like country."

"Clement Greenberg said I looked like an American Modigliani. He wants to have lunch."

"He wants *you* for lunch. They're going to eat you alive. I didn't see him there."

I'd never seen Greenberg so how would I know? But I was beyond the minor inconsistencies for the moment.

"And Phillip Rahv said *Partisan Review* is having a special issue on American Values and would I contribute."

"Will you contribute?"

By now we were probably somewhere down around Hudson Street; a triangular little park, a few benches, less city than Village. She slapped herself down on a

park bench, spreadeagled her long arms on the back
slats, and called out to anyone who would listen:
"It is spring. It's almost three o'clock in the morning.
I've lost a husband and I thought I would die but I
guess I didn't and I'm sorry I never told you before.
But I'm young. I know young people in novels never
say that—but *I'm young* and I've arrived here, but I
haven't quite arrived yet and, yes, oh yes, I will contribute, Katherine is here and whatever the question is
never mind, because the answer right now is, yes, I'll
contribute. *I will contribute!*"

She slipped the shoulders of her dress down with a
rush of unsuspected perfume, as soon as we were inside
the door and the wonderful confusion between sex and
art, between giving and contributing, between mourning
and success began between us. The bed was low, low,
practically just a great mattress on the floor and next
to it as we turned and turned above and below each
other the beat-up Royal portable typewriter trembled
on its little table, trembled as much as we. The insult
of a gulf between the Liberal Imagination and the great
writers of the West did not seem a pressing issue at
that moment. For that moment Katherine was recon-
ciled. She would contribute.

We turned for hours. Once or twice surprise rang in
the air.

"Wonderful . . ."

"What?"

"You—swallowed . . ."

"Is that so special?"

I was not sober enough to chart the geography of my
inexperience.

"It's—very nice . . ."

She rose on an elbow, a dim shape of delight in the
dark.

"Hell," she said and suddenly I heard a Midwestern

music in her voice. "I swallowed in college. Hell's Bells,
I swallowed in high school."

Such, such were the joys which accompanied us to
sleep. I woke panicked. I knew only two things. That
I was finding it hard to breathe and that I had to get
out of there and never come back.

It sounds theatrical, synoptic, as I tell it to you now.
But Katherine's hunger had become, as I slept, a presence, stifling, terrifying. All that energy dedicated to
conquest, *without details.* It was too general; it blanketed
the world. Her grief was too distant for me to handle;
her hope was too pressing. Her innocence was worse
than my father's. By yielding to me in the drunken
coda to the Trilling party she'd involved me in some
extended rape, some violation of which tonight's episode
was only a part. She would swallow and be swallowed
up by the great mouth of New York. All those mouths
with their eloquent tongues forming language, poems,
stories, essays, novels, special issues devoted to Swal-
lowing and Being Swallowed in America—they would
devour Katherine while she devoured them. It was a
contest of cannibals I could not bear to watch or be a
part of.

I dressed in the dark and was out in the hallway in
minutes. That was when I performed the crazy ritual—
what I've thought of ever since as the "desecration." I
took out a large handkerchief and blindfolded myself.
My balance was off and I swayed for a moment, fleeing
that low, low bed into the blindfolded darkness. The
idea itself was simple enough to be comical. I would
protect myself from ever falling back again.

I've told you how complicated the apartment's location was. I knew that if I groped my way down the
stairs and out into the labyrinth of streets and somehow
reached, say, Sheridan Square, without actually seeing

where I was, I'd never find my way back. There was
no phone, we had no friends in common; end of comedy.
All of which tells you that I knew I'd fall back again
if I could. I had little faith in my own detachment. I
tripped over a garbage can and dragged orange rinds,
wet newspaper, and coffee grounds with me for blocks.
"*Desecration . . .*" *To profane that which is sacred.*
Nonsense! Since when is making the beast with two
backs a sacred act?

Turning into the broad acreage of Sheridan Square I
untied the blindfold. Homosexual youths lounged or
prowled; female teachers browsed in an all-night bookstore while their Brooklyn or New Jersey dates debated
the next move. Overhead the building line swam in a
sky of purplish-black; it grew lighter lavender as I
watched. A dwarfish woman was selling balloons. She
pressed a lighted cigarette against three in a row. Pop—
pop—pop! A couple embraced in the doorway next to
me. They made noises while they kissed.

The circus of appetite was in full swing. A dry,
fragrant and cool May night breeze condoned everything
in the world. I turned around, vaguely in the direction
from which I'd come. What a wild yearning I had to
go back! Katherine would still be asleep. I could get
back into bed without waking her up. I would breathe
her breath, berry-fresh. But I had done my desecration
too well. I had no idea which way to go. So I went
home where the telephone was ringing. It was my father.

"I didn't wake you?"

"No."

"It's only 2:30 A.M. here."

"It's only 5:30 A.M. here."

"Listen I want you to help me out."

"How?"

"Talk to your Uncle Harry. He won't give me the
money I need."

"For what?"

"This place is jumping. L.A. loves cars. And the war's over. It's going to be foreign cars . . ."

"Which foreign cars, Dad?"

"I've got a line—"

"How's mother?"

"She's asleep. That's why I'm calling you at this crazy hour, waking you up . . ."

"You didn't wake me up."

"Good. Are you okay?"

"I'm all right."

"Which job are you taking?"

I'd forgotten for days, in my Katherine-haze, that I was to decide on one of the directions my life could take, publishing, advertising; a job in a company. At least I wouldn't be alone. Maybe that's why they called it a "company."

"I haven't decided yet."

"This is expensive . . . talk to your uncle . . . please . . ." I was asleep seconds after hanging up the phone.

If there's a heaven and/or hell with judges and juries, then when my turn comes someone will probably ask me how the Hell I could not think of the pain and humiliation Katherine Eudemie might be feeling. To answer in advance: I don't know. I did not visualize her waking and stretching out a hand and finding the shock of empty space—(you've seen that scene in too many movies; no need to see it here, again). No, I did not let myself think about her feelings of being dropped or abandoned. None of this hurt me then; and it is contemptible that it hurts so much to think of it now.

Feelings are not like buses. If you miss the right one for the right occasion, your ticket is no longer valid. You have no right to the feeling later. It's just regret and self-forgiveness in disguise.

*   *   *

I woke the next morning exhilarated, ready for a new life. To show you how dumb I was I actually thought I'd gained, not lost something. I understood all the mythology of the blind truly seeing—all that stuff I'd long assumed to be bullshit. The blindfold was my new clarity. Fake or authentic, I took it as a gift and used it at once.

I called the editor of the N.Y.U. Press and accepted the extensive copyediting assignment he'd offered: the manuscript on language and sex. What better way to deal with both than behind the disguise of the proof-reader's marks. Publicity and advertising—neither could compete for my detached attention with any authority. I was about to assume the ultimate detached authority: the author's author, if you will, though unacknow-ledged, like Shelley's poets.

It was my answer to Katherine and the demi-gods of the night before. They worshipped the god of language. But from that moment on it was I who would tend his temple, see to it that his lamps had oil, that the right sacrifices were made on the right altars. One of my precisely placed periods would be worth more than a hundred of their ambitious statements about art and life, all giddy with self-love, artful but period-less.

Adding spice to the taste of my choice was the un-derstanding that I would make minimal monies for my pains. It was an answer to everyone in my world at once: my father, my uncle (who'd refused my plea in spite of the imminent explosion of foreign cars on the West Coast) and, most of all Katherine and all of you (though I knew none of you, yet) with all your concerns of language and who and what is central and peripheral.

The copyeditor is the ultimate bystander: the witness at the accident of literature, testifying: "I saw it happen. The author turned left from the right lane, using lo-cutions long forbidden by written law as well as custom and usage." On lucky occasions I have prevented the accidents, given a willing and flexible author.

It was a new life with a new alphabet to learn. The hieroglyphics of the copyeditor are as arcane as any dead language, but I learned quickly.

I moved into an inexpensive, rent-controlled apartment on West 84th Street and settled down to my determinedly peripheral life. No need to feel sorry for me. One person's periphery is another's center—an endless series of contiguous circles stretching to infinity.

Think of the secrets I've been made privy to. This is not the place to describe to you the extraordinary photographs that came, enclosed by mistake, with the first galleys of a book by a woman writer now being nominated for the Nobel prize. The challenge was for me to get them back to her without appearing to have seen them. It wasn't easy. And think of the gifted people I've been brought in touch with. Though I never write to authors whose books I've edited and liked. Not any more. I once wrote admiringly to Rebecca West; she answered me so bitterly that I felt like a traitor. I wrote to Isaac Bashevis Singer and he answered me in Yiddish. Writing fan letters is a mug's game. Far better to be the invisible, controlling Copyeditor whose hand is everywhere felt and nowhere seen.

In the late fifties I helped Gregory Corso organize the first coffee-shop readings in New York. That was when he was still a tough street kid fresh from his first readings at the City Lights Bookstore and an editor at Dutton asked me to pitch in on poetry. Poetry was going to be important. Years went by as in a dream. Poetry went back to being poetry again—i.e., peripheral. Publication parties became more elaborate. The network of referral-editors I needed to keep a flow of work often resulted in a grateful invitation. It offered a social life of sorts. Ah, the secrets hidden there! Who trashed who's book in the *Times* for what not-so-secret motive of revenge, or envy. How much editorial rewriting actually was done on whose Pulitzer Prize nonfiction book. Who was secretly homosexual—when people were still furtive on that score—but enjoyed attacking openly homosexual authors. It was all a whirling cesspool or it was simply the world, depending on how detached or how involved you were. I chose to think it was the world.

A few years later my father, miraculously, made the Mercedes-Benz the Chevy of Los Angeles. He was rich— no surprise to him. Not having money was a failing which had always astonished him. He immediately divorced my mother and made plans to live forever. The times were ripe for a true believer in money. Money, like art, is made with fervor and luck; but you must have both, one won't do. My father had both and he inherited the earth—well, California anyway. He died, happy, two years later having finally succeeded as an alchemist. The *dreck* had become *gelt*. And I have inherited enough money, barely enough, to keep me cheerfully peripheral for the rest of my life. Not enough to tempt a woman to tempt me. And not quite enough to tease me into wanting much more. The embrace with Katherine was the last authentic one I risked. You didn't know an embrace could be a risk? Well, I have preferred other desecrations: the sensual expertise which can be bought, with no need for blindfolds afterwards.

So I stay safely ensconced in my woven blanket of contempt. It gives warmth in the winter. Spring is another matter. On a leafy, restless April night I met Katherine again, at the Random House party for *Portnoy's Complaint*.

She did not seem one hour older. Only a look of secret fatigue at the corners of her bright blue eyes provided a counterpoint, a sub-text to her tale of stories under consideration, of novels optioned, of grants in the works. We walked for a while in the brownstone East Side twilight.

"I wondered if I'd see you again. I caught a glimpse of you," she said. "At Joe Fletcher's funeral. When you spoke."

"Yes," I said.

"People think New York is hard. But it's so soft on spring evenings. That other evening was as soft as could be."

"Ah," I said. "*That* was some evening." I was scared stiff she would plunge right back and of course she did at once.

"I kept thinking you'd call me . . ."

"There was no phone . . ."

"Or come by and leave a note . . ."

I took a breath. It was the moment to do it, to tell her, to purge myself. I would trade her the silly, terrible story of the blindfold and in return she would laugh, forgive me, and make me young again—young in the way she still was.

"It was all too much for me," I said. "I was confused. All those heavy hitters. I kept thinking I'd run into you."

Those blue eyes did their clouding-up routine again, much as I remembered.

"It's just as well," she said. "I was falling in love with you. Now I'm married to Jackson Eudemie and we're trying to have a baby. He was there that night at the Trillings."

"I remember. But he's not Jewish."

"Well—he's in publishing."

"Yes. I did a project with him once."

I got away with it, but barely. The story of the blindfold was still buried in my chest. I was alone with it, again. She paused on the top step before joining the buzz of self-promotion behind her.

"You know what really hurt—really got to me—was not your disappearing act. It was a feeling I had that you were siding with *them* . . . all the big guys and their awful ideas. I mean have you ever *read* Eliot and closed your ears to his song? All of them . . .? The ugliness, the pessimism, the anti-Semitism . . .? For a long time I couldn't figure out where to place you and your vanishing, Trilling and his questions, my poor Doug—you know, my husband—bleeding to death in northern France where people vacation now when they're bored with southern France. I read Trilling's book when it came out . . . *The Liberal Imagination* . . . He felt he had to question everything. But I haven't changed. My heart is still in the right place. I believe we're going to do it—somehow. We're not going to bleed to death until we're all white and papery. We're going to make it all work."

Now it was her turn to vanish.

In 1968 I was jammed among Norman Mailer, Robert Lowell, Isak Dinesen—who was too old to be there or dead at the time—and Aaron Asher in front of the Pentagon and I broke my glasses. I borrowed a pair from a nearby fellow demonstrator and suddenly I saw Katherine and Jackson Eudemie a few yards away. She was holding a baby swathed in blue scarves. That was the last time I saw either of them until last week.

I walked into Jackson's study. His eyes were rimmed pink but he also wore a velvet smoking jacket out of a Somerset Maugham story; he smoked a pipe and rose from a large stuffed chair at the side of a fireplace blaze borrowed from Dickens. He was reading a book—he put it down to greet me and I could read the title. It was actually called—*The Rise and Fall of the Man of Letters*. He was giving me all my cues. No need for us to catch up. I was whatever extreme gesture of detachment I had rehearsed over the years and he was his own parody. Our situation, too, had its own echoes: the widower sending for the former lover. The only original turn here was this insane request for me to speak a eulogy. We talked for a few moments about many years, telescoping events, getting everything muddled but establishing some kind of contact. I told him how impressed I was that Katherine had stuck out her writing career—even though she'd never published a second book. He opened the door to her study. On a large, strong desk lay five boxes in which typing paper once came.

"There they are," Jackson said. His pipe puffed white coded symbols. "Five long serious novels, each with their heart firmly in the right place. Unpublished."

I stared at him.

"**S**he told me—over and again, sometimes laughing, sometimes as if she wasn't sure who the joke was on— she told me your line about being a writer and the problem of having your heart in the right place . . ." He closed the door quietly, as if protecting some obscure privacy. The pipe came out of his bearded mouth and into his hand for emphasis.

"I'd tell her 'Katherine, it comes and goes. One decade brings revolutions, another one brings war, another brings back the private life. Another one is obsessed with health and money. It all revolves. Patience.' " He took me downstairs in front of his literary props. I drank one of them—a snifter of brandy, as we sat in front of another—the fire.

"But she wouldn't have it," Jackson said. "She thought if you gave up innocence, love, democracy, hope, justice—if you gave them up once—even for a minute—

they'd be lost forever." He sighed. "Now it's she who's lost forever."

"Don't be glib," I said. I had no right to speak like that but I was fighting for myself as well. "She didn't die of liberalism, she died of cancer. Why do you want me of all people to speak at the funeral?"

That was when he gave me that awful reply. Recently friends had mentioned that they'd been to this or that funeral—an exiled Cuban poet; a young pianist; a famous woman biographer. And he'd heard—get this— he'd heard that I was *good!*

"Good—what?" I said.

"Good—you know—good."

"Good—how?"

He grew exasperated.

"For God's sake how clear can I be? You were good. You did it well."

"Well!" I said. "How the hell can a funeral oration, a eulogy, be something you can do *well?* Okay, okay," I muttered. "If you're a clergyman, a Rabbi Priest Minister maybe. They're pros. You smoothly get from Part A—the loving family left behind to Part B—the living legacy of love left by the—here comes Part C—the extraordinary benevolent character of the deceased— But a friend, a lover, ex or not, how can you sing a song of personal feeling about someone you've cared about, in such a way that it can be for Christ and Moses' sake—*graded:* good, as opposed to poor or perhaps first-rate or mediocre."

"Bullshit," Jackson said. I'd stung him out of the Man of Letters pose. "You can do anything well or badly."

"Ah," I said. "The famous New York Ethic of Skill— goes hand-in-hand with the Ethic of Success. Everything grist for the mill. I can see the special issue of *New York Magazine* now: The Year's Top Ten Eulogies From The Seven Lively Arts."

"Exactly wrong," he said, stung so badly that he told me a tale of a different Katherine; not steadfast, but on the verge of crack-up for years. Not the Saint of Art I'd thought she was. She had raged at her rejections—bit at her blocks like an infuriated animal; denigrated her contemporaries not for their values but for their success. A picture of the classic middle-aged woman writer—come on the scene too late for the modernist voice, too early for the feminist, with no true voice of her own. The collapse had been total. Last year she'd gone to the bathroom without realizing her clothes were still on. The psychiatrist she'd consulted would be at the funeral.

She'd had lunch at the Russian Tea Room with her agent, taking her baby along because the sitter had not shown up—and had forgotten the baby in the coat room; had not remembered, in the aftermath of the disappointments of the lunch table, for two-and-a-half hours that she had come with a child and left only with her sense of failure. When she got back to the restaurant the waiters were feeding the baby sour cream and no one had called the police. They knew she'd come back. Nobody understood why she wept so, inconsolable. Everyone knew she would do it again.

It was not a story I wanted to hear, not a picture I wanted to see. To block it out, to deflect it, I said, "Stop this crap and tell me why you want me to speak, you lying son-of-a-bitch, me instead of any of the people she'd spent her life with. I knew her for a few weeks, years ago." He looked at me blurred, teary, defenses and poses gone.

"Because I never understood her. You're not married. You don't know about being with someone for year after year and having the feeling that there's one thing you're missing; one key that would explain everything. Of course, in between you're convinced that both of you have exhausted *all* surprise for each other. But with Katherine there was always that mysterious edge: she knew it confused me. I used to call it her shadow-Jew that she carried with her, everywhere. And you"— he swayed next to me as if he were going to fall on me and crush me. Jackson is quite large. I realized that he'd not been to sleep much since Katherine had died. And that had been three days before. Gentiles don't rush their dead into the ground the way Jews do. He was on the edge of collapse. "You—" he said. "I always thought you knew something about what had happened to her when she first came to town. You knew something or *were* something which happened to her. And now is the last chance I'll get to find out. It sounds crazy— okay, but I wanted to find out at the last possible moment what that shadow-Jew was she carried with her."

There was no reason to stay any more. I started to leave.

"You know," he called after me, desperately, "it was suicide."

"Bullshit," I said. "But I'll do it. I'll call you for the time and place."

And this is the time and the place and now we must end this Ending. Since I am Rabbi, Minister, Priest, all rolled up into none—I have written a few words of exhortation: the way I would end Katherine's eulogy if I were to deliver it.

I've seen a generation, your generation, give up its one and only chance. I wonder if it's inevitable. Does every generation make the same movements? I've seen you go from hating injustice to feeling badly treated; from cosmic rage to irritability; from the tragic view of life to merely feeling depressed; from the struggle for truth to the skirmish of advantage. Your Long March towards The Promised Land and Self-Knowledge has brought you to nothing but the psychiatrist and the podiatrist.

As I look around this chapel I feel glad that I have not been included in your text. Life is cleaner in the margins.

I've told the story of the blindfold, of the desecration, and since only saints pray for others while the rest of us pray for ourselves, please rise and join me in the following prayer:

Come back Katherine Eudemie, come back beautiful and sturdy wheat-shaded girl of my one and only chance. Come back and let's leave the party together again. Let's walk once more down Morningside Heights, past the dark and oily river, along the tranquil streets still safe-guarded by the Liberal Imagination, walk all the way down to the haven of the Village. Come back and undress again in the half-darkness and make love and be made love to in the glow of excited, unsatisfied ambition, turning, turning, in the low, low bed next to the trembling table bearing the Royal Portable, you trembling under me, me trembling under you; come back and let me, this time, lie next to you all night— what's left of it—blindfolded only by darkness and sleep till morning wakes us both with all the wonderful and awful obligations of love and light.

THE INTERPRETATION OF DREAMS BY SIGMUND FREUD

a story

"Always a threesome," she said. "Two men and a woman. Except that one man, the one with previous rights in the matter, is always dead."

"I hate this nickel analysis," he said.

"I can't help it. When it gets neat is when it feels true. You don't have to *do* anything about it. It's just that it's like a murder mystery with a series of imaginary murders. If you marry two widows there are two dead men in the background."

This is how it went after his second wife was bitten on the finger by a squirrel, Dickstein had a feeling things would change, and not for the better. It was a three-month situation: meeting, wooing, marrying, and up to New York for a new life. She was fourteen years younger than he and nothing besides falling in love and marriage had been decided. Would she work at her music, at a job, have a baby, have two babies? In the meantime it was a muggy August and against his wishes—though he hadn't examined them or actually expressed them—she had been marking time taking a course at the N.Y.U. Summer School: "Dream, Myth and Metaphor."

The day had been warm and after class she'd lingered in a small rainbow of sunlight and offered one of the peanuts she was shucking and munching to a begging squirrel. She was a Georgia girl and the peanut habit died hard.

Fortunately, after the animal nipped her and drew blood a sharp park attendant netted the squirrel. The rabies test was negative but they put the little bastard

35

to sleep anyway. Leaving Sharon in bed for a few days with shock and a bandaged hand.

"You're mad at me," she said to Dickstein.

"Surprised," he said. "What happened to your country girl smarts? You don't feed New York squirrels from your hand."

"Well, how would I learn that in Chapel Hill?"

He snapped a portable dinner tray in place and tried a laugh. "I always thought that course was dangerous."

"How so?"

He shut up fast. There was no decent way he could tell her how he'd felt the day she came back from the class with a paperback copy of Freud's *Interpretation of Dreams*. Tell her what? That if he'd wanted to marry somebody who could rattle off about latent and manifest content, who could play peek-a-boo with symbols and wish-fulfillment and repression he wouldn't have waited until he was thirty-nine to remarry. He could have tied up with any of the smart-ass, overeducated, under-serious women he'd spent most of his life with.

Sharon was wonderfully articulate without being glib. She had the southern gift for language flow without the little chunks of undigested information—okay, call it knowledge—that was the conversation he'd grown up with and hated. He couldn't tell her any of this because it would come out upside down. The truth of it was in intangibles: the intelligence of her smile, the quick wit that sparkled questions the night he'd lectured to a dozen students who'd swallowed a snowstorm just to hear him compare Shubert and Keats.

"They both go from major to minor keys and back again very quickly," she'd said. Not a question or academic comment: a fragment of song. Just what he was in need of: idea-tossed, song-hungry. "I mean," he said, "that I expected you to start poking at yourself with the new tools of psychology."

"Instead," she said. "I'm poking at you."

"Can you have wine?" he asked. "I forgot what the doctor said."

Sharon shivered against her pillows. "He didn't say. I'll have a glass, thank you. Listen, you knew I was a widow, right off."

"You told me instantly. With all the appropriately southern Gothic details."

"Gothic! It was a hunting accident. Everybody in our part of Georgia hunts. But you didn't tell me your first wife—Alma—was a widow until, for God's sake, last week!"

"It didn't seem important. It's all of three months, not our golden wedding anniversary. Both men died natural deaths—one, sickness, one a shooting accident—both men were considerably older than the women. Now you know what I know."

Dickstein filled the bowls with linguine and shared the wine.

"Two widows," she sighed.

"I'm damned if I know why I didn't tell you sooner. But you didn't notice anything odd until New York University and Sigmund Freud told you it was worthy of thinking about."

He set down an amazement of utensils any which way on the trays. It was not like him and he noted it.

"It gave me the shivers," she began . . .

"What did?"

"Reading the dream book. I think you have to read things at the right moment for them to get to you. I must have read Freud at school. I took all the right courses. I graduated. I took a year of graduate school."

"You were doing music, not psychology."

"But reading this now in class it gave me the eerie feeling that everything is connected."

"Overdetermined . . ."

"Please don't be just clever," she said. "I'm wounded and I'm trying to track something down. I got shaky in class and that's why I wasn't careful in the park . . . It wasn't a change in the way I think—I wasn't born yesterday. It was a weird change in the way I *feel* about the way I think."

"Let me see; is that oozing?"

"Looks the same. I've been bitten before."

"Not in Washington Square Park. City animals are more dangerous."

She ate carefully with her left hand.

"I'm talking about the sensation of strangeness—just thinking that causes and connections run through everything like the bloodstream through the body."

"Did you think everything was random, till yesterday?"

She laughed. "I *felt* that way till yesterday. Then, sitting on the bench with the bag of peanuts I got distracted, the wet heat, I'm used to more hot and dry in August, and I began to think about you and Alma and me and Joshua and widows and husbands and fathers and wives and mothers, and it was more like a dream than *thinking* and I fed this squirrel and I must have done it in a funny way because I've fed them a million times before and nothing ever happened and he bit me."

Dickstein didn't know why the memory appeared for delivery at that moment. It was not a buried one, was right at hand. Rather, it showed up at that instant to help deal with Sharon, who sounded shakier every minute.

"To give you a dose of strange," he told her, "You're not my second widow. You're my fourth. You're living with a regular Bluebeard in reverse."

And he told her of being puppy-young, meeting the war widow with the long legs at a fundraising chamber music evening, and about his family's terror. His father, Dr. Dickstein, the gynecologist/philosopher and his Big Moment in Paternal Wisdom!

"A woman whose husband has died and who marries a younger man puts too much of a burden on the boy. And don't forget: she'll always be comparing you to him."

So he was shipped out to Stanford instead of finishing at Columbia and fell in love, for a time, with a California aerospace widow. Nothing glamorous like a test-pilot crash; just an equipment explosion.

"It's not funny," Sharon said; she was purplish from trying not to laugh. His intent was distraction and seemed to be succeeding. She was slipping into her country accent as she did when she felt easier. She wasn't a modern West-Side-of-New-York Sharon; her full name was Rose-a-Sharon. "I grieved so much," she said, "when Joshua died. I was mad, too, 'cause I hated hunting."

"We're not talking about how it feels when your husband dies. We're talking about how much more connective tissue there is here than even you thought of."

She wasn't laughing anymore. "Four," she murmured. "A daytime dream of the dream. The older man who possesses your woman first dies, but you didn't kill him. You just get to have her. Over and over again. My God. Doesn't that count as murder and possession of the spoils?"

What he couldn't bring himself to bring up was what would seem to be the underlying strategy. He saw all these men as brutal, himself as tender; they were heedless of their women, he was concerned; they took what they wanted, he asked or waited for the moment to ripen.

When Dickstein envisioned those hunting trips of Sharon's husband, Joshua, he imagined some kind of secret, violent sex mixed in with the country satisfactions of blood sport. He'd never asked her about such things and she'd not offered much beyond a black mustache, six-foot-three height and a paper mill business. Questions of fidelity were not included in the data. But when he recalled his father's caution, he welcomed the comparison. Not only were they dead and he alive: *he was molded to offer precisely what they lacked. That was his enterprise!*

But he wasn't going to bring up all that and reinforce this dream-book talk. Instead, he poured the wine more freely than usual and the astonishment turned festive. Sharon was pretty in what she called her sick-time-of-the-month robe, though only her finger bled. They laughed again at her fears of the "uncanny" connections in the mind. (Freud, he told her, had written a famous letter in which he claimed an absence of any such "uncanny" feelings; more about religion than psychology, though.) And she promised never to feed squirrels in the city, again—and she grew coy and sensual, drinking more and eating less, holding her injured hand out into the air as she caressed him with the other and it seemed like a nice idea to eat dinner in the bedroom at times and afterwards she asked him if she were the more precious of the prizes he'd won from the dream-murder of all those father/lovers; and he kissed her mouth as answer and evasion and she grew most southern and promised to at least consider dropping the class since something about it bothered him, if he would take her to Turkey at Christmas-time. (He had absolutely no interest in things Turkish.)

She wondered aloud if they'd made a baby; and he wondered, silently, thinking he could be a husband and a father and could die, like all the others, leaving his lovely Rose-a-Sharon for . . . who?

Late that night he woke, his head frantic from too much wine. In the bathroom he stared at the mirror and thought of his father's face for the first time in many months: square-immigrant-tough where Dickstein's was second-generation soft-nurtured; perfunctory and commanding with his sullen, witty wife, where Dickstein was the one who provided attentions and the occasions for laughter. He remembered the early childhood Saturday visits to Dr. Dickstein's office, the women waiting patiently, obediently, and the chrome and the stirrups . . . and remembered, too, years later, how amazed he was that the old man should be at the mercy of the pain and fears which came with final illness. He'd never seen his father at the mercy of anything before.

Dickstein's eyes blazed in the bathroom mirror with the awful knowledge that there were no more of these imposing older men to die and leave him their women to take for his own. He would be forty in three months, he thought, and listened to Sharon's regular hiss of breath. Now he was at the top of the ladder: an uncomfortable, precarious position.

There she lay, the next widow, unsuspecting; in spite of her squirrel-wisdom, in spite of N.Y.U. and Freud. Because she was young and easy in her skin and had been bereaved only by a rifle, not by time and entropy.

"Peasant pleasures," his father would have said, with irony, about people who died in hunting accidents. He'd sent himself through college and sold insurance to help pay for medical school. These successes entitled him to a loftiness towards those less educated and less successful. Including, on occasion, his wife and son. But now Dickstein, staring into the mirror, saw mirror-images hard to ignore. He, too, had become a Dr. Dickstein, though only a Ph.D. shadow of the real thing: no chrome, no stirrups, not even a white coat.

Like his father, he always had at least three major activities. (The old man lectured, did the first television medical education series along with his regular practice.) Dickstein taught English, lectured when asked, and edited a journal.) The income and prestige were not comparable but the restless multiple activities had similar outlines.

He searched in the mirror for some of the older man's features he could recognize and endow with the qualities he admired. What he thought of as Hungarian; a mouth he saw as eloquent, romantic.

"The better for talking out of both sides at the same time," Dr. Dickstein had said, laughing his runaway laugh. Dickstein, too, laughed nonstop, large and loud. For years he'd felt his father's heavy laughter aimed at him. The truth was, he suspected, that it was aimed at everyone, the good doctor included.

But that was all gone. It was utterly quiet in the night. He sat on the closed commode and leaned his flushed face against the tile of the sink.

"The top of the ladder," he whispered. And now it was not some young woman waiting to greet him. It was his father, waiting where vanished fathers wait for sons.

The disturbing image mixed with the wine in his gut in a surprise of nausea. He vomited into the sink with an energetic heave. It lasted several minutes and then he fell asleep wedged against the sink, the water still running.

Sharon found him about ten minutes after dawn. He was slumped over the sink. When she touched his shoulder, instead of jumping he woke gradually, her lovely cloud of yellow-reddish hair swimming into vague, then focused view. Her eyes and cheeks looked slept-in, striated, rumpled.

She had to pee and he tottered to his feet and waited. When she finished she washed the sink and sat him down again and washed his face with her good hand. He had the convalescent's quiet gladness that she was present, that she had found him, that he had found her.

She would undoubtedly survive him. That was in the natural order of things. But first, for as long as possible, they would survive together. He would be her loving husband, father, friend, teacher: wise, sensual, patient; knowing that, like all teachers, he was temporary.

And for himself, he would learn to ward off the inevitable, to slow down the dance of death. It was time to become his own father: forgiving, intelligent, always remembering that he had once been young and lost and now was found.

A new arrangement.

The bathroom smelled of vomit and Sharon sprayed something lilac into the air and gave him something mint to rinse his mouth with and kissed him and stumbled back to bed and sleep.

Dickstein sat there a moment. He had never felt so lucky in his life.

It was like a dream.

A CLEAN WELL-LIGHTED PLACE
BY ERNEST HEMINGWAY

a story

Of course there were the ones I went back to whenever I was in a certain city, the special ones in which to spend time, like Harry's Bar in Venice where Marcello Mastroianni had once lazily intruded into a private conversation I was having with an Italian film director, a small bar seating no more than eight, maybe nine, which was forever associated in the mind with success and money and a certain sentimental history of earlier decades. Until one bad night when Noah was kept waiting for two hours by the younger Cipriani, Noah who always offered loyalty and expected betrayal and who when wounded clamped his scarred jaw tighter than usual which was very tight and that bar then became simply a stylish place to be crowded and a place for Noah to order his Bellinis and to reminisce about which table this or that great writer had commanded; angry at himself for being concerned, for being trivial ("That's what I've come to," he said. "Restaurant tables . . . percentages of box office revenues—they're what people like me have instead of battlefields, instead of codes of honor. Ridiculous stuff, boy." Calling me boy even though I was only six years younger.)

And years later when I'd gotten into that trouble about the money, which changed everything, and when there were no more Italian film directors in my life, Harry's was a tourist place because I was now only a tourist in Italy. Unlike, say, the Bar at the Oak Room in New York, which also seated many more people and where I'd left a good part of my hopeful youth, trying out schemes, ideas, running up tabs, breaking up with women before they could break up with me. I was going for a degree at the N.Y.U. Film School, or at least that was the idea my parents had, in Madison, Wisconsin, where the checks came from. But the real idea was to hang out at the Oak Room in the reflected gleam of writers, directors, and film producers like Noah, except there really were no others quite like Noah. And even though it was attached to a hotel which hung out flags when visiting heads of state were asleep upstairs, you could never be a tourist at a place where that much had gone on between the drinks.

It was where I first tasted the pleasures of bright, bitter-cold vodka hitting on an empty stomach at a clean, dark wood-lacquered bar, sometimes no one but the bartender and me in the mysterious city light of five in the afternoon, different of course at different seasons; that and my own heightened sense of possibility even though I was broke and couldn't figure out how to go more than ten months with the same woman, still that particular bar gave me the special sense of being freer than other people. Hard to explain, trapped as I was in my helpless youth and confusion, nursing that helplessness like the one drink I could afford. I was austere, too—content to share the space with the bartender, not speaking to him, and I still do not trust people who chat with bartenders, except for Noah. I know, I know there is a grand literary tradition of bartender-conversations but I find something finally patronizing in it.

So I would hold my silence with various aids, a book, a cigarette, a notebook, or all three, until Noah arrived to sit beside me, drink in hand, evanescent deal pending, perilous film project in the works, Noah arriving with his European-acquired irony, "Vodka on the rocks and no small talk for my young friend," Noah said and raised his Bellini in a mock toast to my famous integrity. "Small talk can lead to lies and that rhymes with compromise." At that time he was engaged in a series of warnings about what it might take from me in order to survive the world—if I decided to join it. The world was not the neat university town of Madison, Wisconsin—snow-white and tenured with ski-slopes of professorial parents and a Ph.D. thesis on the films of Jean Renoir. The world was commercial employment in which one was bought and was sold, the world was marriage, the world was The Industry, none of which I'd yet experienced first-hand.

"You're not set up for real life," he told me. "You're young and you own some time to swim around in. You'd better tread water for as long as you can. Above all, stay away from people who produce movies. They swim by different rules. You just tread water."

"How about you?"

"I've told you—the men in my family don't live past fifty-five." He had, indeed, told me, at various hours of the bar-nights. It was not something you checked into too carefully at those moments. Something held me back from asking how old Noah was at this moment. Instead all I said was, "I don't trust your cynicism."

"Never use any word ending with i-s-m."

Being older, he played the teacher. I played the rebellious student, ready to give up the straight path set out for me since childhood. By his cynicism I meant that he kept things back; there was a hollow beneath his sentences. I put in everything I meant when I spoke. He left things out.

Also, there was his World War II scarred jaw, which no one dared to ask about and there was his despairing insomnia. One night at that tiniest of bars at La Colombe D'Or in St. Paul de Vence, he told me about the sleeplessness. It was a bar where you sat at the window if you were lucky and got the right seat and could look out at the lovely garden with the formidable Leger built into the wall, and where I was producing an interview for RAI Television in Rome with a very political French movie star—(my first small try at entering The World, The Industry). The star was a man Noah wanted to interest in his obsession, a movie of a Hemingway's short story called "A Clean Well-lighted Place."

The French actor had said only, "But this is a four-page story. How can it be a movie?"

"Look at *The Killers.* Burt Lancaster, Ava Gardner. How long is long, monsieur?"

"What?" the actor said.

"Nada," Noah said, "Nada, nada, nada . . ."

He was being rude, not usual for him and had not even drunk much. Perhaps he was putting on a small show of bristly integrity for me since I had, in the interval between the bar in New York and the one in St. Paul, started to join the world of buying and selling. The being bought and the being sold were still in the future.

That night, slowly sipping his last drink—the bar didn't exactly close since it was also part of the hotel's lobby but the bartender had long since gone to bed—Noah was guilty at having behaved badly but rather proud of having taken a stand on the issue of Scale in Art. He was sad, too, after another defeat for his special project and spoke about his sleeplessness so as not to speak about other things.

"Can you imagine," Noah said, "a four-year-old being kept awake night after night by the perfectly perceived sense that everything is nothing—*nada?* Existential, infantile insomnia. I've not slept a night through since. You can see why I fell in love with this smallest of Hemingway stories when I came on it years later."

"He hadn't even read "The Killers"!" I said. "Do you think your not sleeping as a child had to do with what you said about the men in your family dying young?"

"I never said that," Noah said coolly. "I said that they didn't live very long, none of them."

I did not make an issue of what he had said or had not said. "Your father?" I said. "Was he alive when you were four?"

"Oh, my God," Noah said in despair. "Yes. But not for much longer. Not long enough. And don't ask me how much is enough."

"Unkind," I said.

"I guess so. Blame it on your friend the actor. He got to my nerves. Actors!" Noah said. "You and me," he added, "We're like the two waiters in the Hemingway story," and when I pressed him to explain he hid behind his glass. "Remember in Venice," he said with apparent irrelevance, "how Cipriani kept me waiting two hours for a table?"

"Why did you wait?" I asked.

"I had to play it out. He was an old friend and it was one of the places where I'd spent my time and something was up. You have to play things out. It's part of the game."

As soon as I got back to Rome after I deposited my film at the R.A.I. Lab I went to the little English language paperback book store at the foot of the Spanish Steps. I found a copy of Hemingway's short stories and read "A Clean Well-lighted Place." It was a fine story, condensed, lyrical, as much poem as story, since the shadows which leaves make against electric light are invoked as image and consolation and since the two waiters who are the main characters talk the way no two waiters have ever talked, especially the older waiter.

Nevertheless, in it I saw my friend Noah, or at least I saw what he saw in this simple story: in a small café,

probably in Spain, late at night, an old deaf man who
has tried to kill himself the week before is drinking
brandy and keeping two waiters from closing up. The
younger waiter is cold and confident, irritated with the
old man and his miseries and his comrade's anxieties
about *nada*—the nothing surrounding everything. The
older one is sympathetic and uncertain. Their conflict
appears to be about whether they should hurry the old
man out of the café—it is two-thirty in the morning—
or let him drink for another hour. The younger waiter
has a wife waiting at home in bed.

The older waiter says, "I am of those who like to
stay late at the café . . . with all those who need a
light for the night . . ." The younger waiter does not
understand. The word *nada* means nothing to him. We
are left with the older waiter and an unclear dread
against which one can only place the need for light and
a certain cleanliness and order. At the end the older
waiter offers a parody of the Lord's Prayer and the
prospect of grappling with the dread that keeps one
awake until daylight. "After all," he said to himself, it
is probably only insomnia. Many must have it."

"I've read your Hemingway story," I told Noah. "I
see why you're so high on it."

"You're not supposed to see that," he said. "You're
the younger waiter."

"No imagination . . . ?"

"No sense of the danger of ordinary life. But you're
not thirty yet. You can still take it easy for a while."

"Tread water?"

"That's the idea."

Then I told him, "Ivan wants me to do a project with
him."

We were in Berlin, having a drink at the Kempinski,
an awful spread-out, lobby sort of affair, but it was
where the Berlin Festival people all stayed. I was on

sabbatical; my little film on the French actor had been entered in the festival, had won nothing, but I had been noticed. That felt like winning.

"Ivan," Noah said. "My God, he's going to start with Ivan. You never go by the book, do you?"

It was an old complaint. I'd never done anything by the rules . . . I played the piano passably well but only by ear . . . I went to three colleges which is to say none that I ever completed . . . I played tennis with the club pros but I had my own weird service and no topspin.

"Ivan," Noah said. "I've had to do with Ivan a few times." I was supposed to understand everything from that. And then, "Playing with Ivan the one thing that might be worse than losing—is winning."

Years passed, more than a decade, marked by the confusion of work—even of love. I made a good deal of money but kept little of it and was married once and kept little of it, not even a child. Ivan and I had some success. It became important for me to realize how different I was from Noah. I didn't want to tread water while he swam the mysterious Industry Crawl. I didn't want to play young waiter to his older one. Yet *nada* was nothing to me. That part was accurate. I had always slept well. Perhaps because the men in *my* family have always lived into their eighties. Chronic low blood pressure.

Even when I got into the tight spot that changed everything—I took money from the production budget to cover personal expenses—even after Ivan found out and the L.A. District Attorney's office came into it—I slept well. And when it became clear that I was not going to go to jail, even though everything was now changed, my only regret was Noah. He'd borrowed some money from me; some trouble with one of his children had found him short of cash. And I was concerned that something pure in Noah, something clean and well-lighted, might worry that he had unknowingly borrowed stolen money.

We had it out one evening in L.A. It started over vodka Gibsons at Chasen's. There was a waiting line even if you had a reservation and I could tell Noah was not at his most patient that evening. I couldn't tell if it was being kept waiting, or just L.A. itself, in which Noah never felt comfortable. Perhaps it was me and the scrape I'd just gotten out of.

"I guess you're not going to have any real trouble about it," he said.

"Well, they're not going to press it hard."

"Too many of Ivan's friends have done worse."

"I don't need a whitewash," I said."

"We need a table. But in the meantime let me say that I am glad you will stay free—I cannot envision you in jail—and I am not going to mention it again."

An hour and a half later we were both in the L.A. County Jail. Noah's edge had gotten sharper and sharper as the line got longer. Finally the headwaiter stood an inch too close to Noah while telling him the usual lies about how long the wait would be and Noah hit him. He didn't push him away—he hit him. We'd both been drinking more than usual—I've noticed you drink more standing up than sitting down—and we'd been kept standing too long. Also, I'd been waiting for months to

find out if I was going to prison and Noah had been
waiting to find the true story and then the line at the
restaurant—one delay too many.

"Well," Noah said, amused at last that evening, "interesting place."

"Unexpected."

"Thus interesting."

"Ivan's lawyer was trying to make it quite interesting
until we all agreed on things. But here I am in jail,
anyway," I said.

"But thanks to me, no thanks to you," Noah said.
"I'm used to places like this."

"You?"

"Well, not lately and not real jail—Army jail . . ."
And he told me the story of the snowy weeks in Bastogne
before the big German attack and how his redneck
sergeant got the fixed idea that Noah was a Jew and
that it was important for Noah to admit it or deny it.
Noah would not tell the son-of-a-bitch that he was part
Indian and part Lutheran and the sergeant found many
excuses to jail Noah for this or that offense but finally
they had to fight it out the day before the German
attack came. And they rolled on the floor of the latrine
and even though Noah was losing—or so he said—the
sergeant pulled a knife on him, slashed his face, and
at least Noah got to go home.

By the time he finished the story I was quite sober
but he seemed still high, sitting in the stone corner of
the cell waiting for my lawyer to find us.

Something in me, though, was not sober, not quieted.
Being white middle-class citizens we were not really
in jail. My lawyer was at home when I called, so we
were in jail as much as if we had been in a car accident

in some ambiguous circumstances. We spent an hour
and a half in a vast grimy waiting room—but it wasn't
much different than the big, wooden-benched waiting
rooms you see on jury duty. It was not prison to people
who might have to know prison. Oddly, the only specific
details I remember are a puddle of indeterminate origin
at the entrance to the waiting room, the extraordinary
surreal height of the judge's desk, and a man in a grey
pin-striped suit with a vest, who read a newspaper with
great calm. I assumed he was a lawyer but when he
stood up and was taken away I saw that he was hand-
cuffed to the policeman who'd been sitting next to him.

Later, in the Polo Lounge Bar I said: "Okay, now I
know how you got that scar."

"Okay, now you know."

"That sounds like there's something much more important that I don't know."

"I'm sorry I hit the waiter."

"He wasn't a waiter. It was very important to him
that he wasn't a waiter." I said.

"Don't do that, boy," Noah said. "I don't need any
credit for hitting him. It was a dumb thing to do. And
I don't need any credit for being cut by the sergeant
in France, either."

"My God," I said. "How did we land there, in such
a place?" I shook my head.

"We didn't," he said. "We're here, drinking brandy."

"True . . ."

"We never actually land anyplace," Noah said. His
voice was a little too loud for the bar, the evening, the
circumstance. "We don't live in places."

"Oh?"

"We live in time. One of the best-kept secrets. Middle-class nomads all. Think of all those cities—and if you're in a city that is not your one city it becomes a matter of hotels and bars. Now if you'd stayed in Madison, Wisconsin, where—" His sip gave me license to interrupt.

"Where my father and mother live their lives—their places . . ."

"At least Ivan never shows up in Wisconsin. The trouble might never have happened."

"It didn't happen. I *did* it! I took the money. And it took being kept waiting for a table to make you hit me with it."

"No," Noah said. "No, no, no, I never used it and I won't now . . ." But something made me sorry that Noah had told me about the sergeant and the scar. I don't know exactly why but they seemed connected to the intense words about place and time which had given way to a simple reproach for having become, for a brief moment in a careless way—a thief.

"I'm just as bad," Noah said. "What you lose is the starting place. Maybe that's why it pissed me off so much, Cipriani keeping me waiting—Harry's was one of my homes—and that's a stupid confession to have to make, that a bar or a restaurant can be like a true place."

He waited long enough for me to contradict him. Or long enough for me to realize that the poor maitre d' at Chasen's had received the punch begun in Venice so long ago. When I said nothing he put his glass down and stood up. It was the first time I saw him unsteady on his feet. He looked down at me, somehow disappointed. Perhaps because I'd gone so far away from my starting place. But that may have been only my regret of the night pasted onto Noah.

"My place," he said, "is that little Hemingway story. A Clean Well-Lighted Place . . ."

I was disgusted.

"Balls," I said. "You haven't even got that story straight."

"It's hard to get stories straight," Noah said. "But at least mine is small, cut down to scale . . . Four pages . . . an old, suicidal drunk and two waiters one young and confident, one old and uncertain . . ."

"Uncertain, sleepless," I said. I knew what I was doing. "*Because all the men in his family die young.* That's crap . . ."

"It doesn't matter if it is," Noah said, "my young friend . . ." His old familiar tone was back for a moment. "It's all part of my story. Maybe you should get yourself a story."

"I thought I was in yours," I said and moved my hand, almost invisibly, for the check. I wanted this to be over. Noah looked strange.

He said: "If a story is the only place left, then we sing our songs for ourselves, past present and sometimes there's more pain in a pop song than a sergeant's knife . . ."

I listened coldly, never having seen or heard Noah out of control before, as if the simple fact of hitting a headwaiter and being in a jail again, even so briefly, had broken the skin of old wounds, wounds I would never know about.

". . . the weird light of Los Angeles," he was saying, "though I can't think of a place less likely to invoke angels. Okay, I'll stop the jokes since you're not laughing . . . I'll talk about your soul . . . it lives only in bars because its birthplace has been lost and its destination is not known . . . so instead of a place it has time . . . a bar has closing time a place does not . . ."

"Noah," I said.

"No reason to be embarrassed my friend, or to interrupt . . . I will sleep easily tonight . . . nothing is nothing tonight . . . *nada y nada pues nada* . . . here in the land of billboards plugging new records by new rock groups . . . I don't think it has to do with the making of money or the spending or the very temporary jail . . . it has to do with the permanent absence of a place in our lives, yours and mine . . . (Noah's disjointed monologue was no longer going unnoticed—two young women in hard-glinting metallic dresses were trying not to stare) . . . time is a desert and one is always thirsty in a desert . . . and making movies or money or love is all the same in time . . . and that," Noah paused and touched his eyelids one after the other in mysterious ritual pause, ". . . and that is somehow too equal and easy. Something," he said, "should be wrong . . ."

"Okay," I said. "It's all right, Noah. It's over now." He sat down next to me for a moment, then stood up, restless, nervous again, his face flushed to the tip of his aloof brow. Had I walked in just then I might not have recognized my old companion.

"Don't count on that," he said.

"I'm not."

"I know," he said. "*Nada*." I was tapped out of sympathy, the tirade had exhausted my patience, not quite fair since in decades of bar-meetings Noah's style had always been spare sober, dry as Vermouth. But tonight my body was tired and my eyes ached from looking away.

Having had my fill of this new fantastical Noah, I stood up and beckoned for the waiter. Okay, I thought, I took the wrong road, I took the money and now I can't take this any more. And we left that bar with a brief skirmish in which I insisted that I drive Noah to his hotel and the doorman could have Noah's car brought around in the morning, but Noah said no, he was fine and I drove off first not wishing to see him leave.

*   *   *

We lost track of each other. I fled to Rome; everything seems distant and muted in Rome. All those ruins. Noah's Hemingway movie remained unmade. It was a quixotic notion given the nature of movies, of the story, of Noah. I heard that he was now in the U.S. trying to set up an American production company.

I started hanging out at the bar in the Inghilterra, starting, too, the foolishness of trying to write stories. It was clear I was not going to make any more movies, with or without Ivan. So I haunted the Inghilterra. It was small and dark. The best bars seemed to be getting smaller and darker in spite of Noah and Hemingway. But it was several generations after Hemingway and the consoling darkness of interiors may have replaced the comfort of light, cleanliness, and order.

The Inghilterra bar was too small, because at that time I wanted very much to hide and observe and small places are exposed. But for some crazy reason, after my time with Ivan I wanted to watch writers like Moravia and Calvino come there to drink and argue with their stout publishers in stiff blue suits, white shirts, and dotted ties, dress they wore even in the summer Roman heat, and to watch the writers being interviewed by skinny, sweatered young journalists with portable tape recorders and cigarettes burning forgetfully down to their fingertips, the young people drinking strange semi-alcoholic drinks like Fernet-Branca and the writers drinking highly alcoholic ones like Grappa. No solitude here; no matter how early in the day I showed up there were always patrons; but the action was gentle, literary, about all I could handle in my convalescent condition. It was as if I was borrowing strength to learn how to stay with thinking up stories, learning how to live cheaply and ignore the seductions of money and petty power which had gotten me into trouble in the first place, just as Noah had warned me, and I had to borrow this real or imagined sense of integrity in a small foreign bar among people whose fame and authenticity was heightened by their speaking a language I understood little of but whose music and gestures I loved.

I had money put aside for maybe one year, and after Italy it was going to be France, partly because on a quick trip to Paris I met a woman at the bar at the Pont Royal, where you walk downstairs and it's all somehow terribly serious and formal though it's a long time since someone like Camus drank there. (You don't stay at the hotel upstairs because the hotel people are cold and rude, but the bar is merely cool and there are times when detachment is desirable even essential.) Meeting this woman there—the only time I have ever "picked up" someone at a bar—colored what happened after that. She was just the kind of woman you meet, if luck holds, when the *nada* arrives and feels as if it will stay. It worked out well until one day she accused me of being disappointed; not such a terrible thing to say on the face of it, but not such a good thing either if you felt the way I was feeling.

She told me, too, that I was only concerned with the appearance of things, that I had lost all sense of place in the world, and I thought My God does everyone know that song now, and she told me that the insomnia I was developing was an affectation and we broke up. She had told me, as well, that I spent too much time in bars and that I was not really trying to learn to make stories, only trying to give the appearance of making stories but by that time it was true and she was not to blame for saying it.

Bars are, finally, places of appearance, which means illusion and perhaps that is why so much business is transacted in them; theaters in which the unbilled character is alcohol, sometimes a small character part, sometimes a main role—and that is trouble. But I am getting older and have fears that the drinking, which was never what those places were about for me, might be getting more important and I think with some nostalgia of the foolishly old-fashioned bustle of the bar at 21, if bars were people it would be someone living beyond their means; I think of the Ritz in Madrid, gloomy, hushed, poised with a sense of secret sorrow, and I think of the bright and proper bar at the Connaught in London, where one would not dare have a thought which was too personal.

I think, too, of bars in Hollywood on sunny sad exposed streets, Fountain Avenue or LaBrea, bars with names like the Hopalong or the Tarpit, places in which, even at night, the interior light suggests a depressing late afternoon in which disappointment fills the lines on every face, bars in which miserable men and women sit in stiff and stately failure until drink loosens bones and tongues and evenings end in violence, though sometimes only verbal violence; evenings so many years ago, long before I'd met Noah or myself, when I had lost nothing yet because I'd gained nothing yet, except what I'd brought with me; all that hope.

And the public spaces in which we encounter each other, glasses in hand like magic talismans, cannot help or harm if what Noah said is true—if we have lost our places and are drifting about, unmoored, in time. And finally it is possible to be quite alone in the busiest of bars and sometimes we return home to sleep or lie awake in beds full of uninvited guests.

It ended up in one of the bars neither of us cared for, which doubled as a hotel lobby. At one of those unsatisfactory hybrids I learned that Noah had died. Sitting at a table at the Anglo-Americano in Florence, a small bar in that small city, in a hotel which used to be sweet and awkwardly eager to please and is now smooth and plays host to business conventions, I was told by a German producer who had invited me to discuss returning to the making of money via a lovely movie deal. In the middle of the conversation he'd remembered that I knew Noah and he told me.

To cover my confusion at hearing this from a stranger I said, "Yes, all the men in his family died young."

"What do you mean," the German producer said over his metal-rimmed glasses, "I met his father in New York—he was at least seventy-five and he has an older brother."

To make matters worse he showed me the obituary in the International *Herald Tribune*, which told us all that Noah had "passed away" after a long illness. (He would have been amused at the euphemism—"Which way," he would ask with bursting bladder at a first-time bar, "to the euphemism?") I was glad of this last, strangely, because I'd sometimes been afraid of a much more abrupt end for Noah. He had, after all, come apart that night in Chasen's and had cast himself as the older waiter in the Hemingway story, the waiter who had sympathy for the suicidal old man. But, infantile insomnia notwithstanding, Noah went a draftee not a volunteer into the army of Death.

The German producer went on and on; he knew Noah well, it seemed. He even knew that the scar had a story; only, after dinner and after being joined by a beautiful young woman, thin-boned arched nose, a woman who listened with intent gray eyes, she seemed as delicate as the man was gross, and after a certain amount of wine it seemed that his story of the scar was entirely different, no anti-Semitic sergeant, something about a poker game and an accusation of cheating

and a fight and being sent home before the Battle of
the Bulge, the last part matched all right.

Back in the hotel lobby, formica tables and flourescent
lighting, sterile, successful, relentlessly international,
over a fresh, clean-tasting Poire eau de vie, I tuned him
out; all I could think to do was recite to myself Noah's
and Hemingway's parody of the Lord's Prayer, *Our nada
which art in Nada, nada be thy name* . . .

And I felt the weight of years, of months, of minutes
whose foolish nature was simply to pass, felt this along
with a weird joy at the moments still to come. It was
late at night and the woman was gazing at me sym-
pathetically while the producer kept alternating remi-
niscences of Noah with pieces of the film deal. "I never
met your friend," she said in some accent I could not
place, "but I am sorry."

I would have liked to have dumped the man and
spent the rest of the time telling the beautiful young
woman with sympathetic, oriental eyes about my hopeless attempt to write stories so that one of them could
be mine and would be my place and how that had not
worked out, which was why I was listening to her
friend or lover talk death and deals alternately in Florence.

Instead, before the evening finished I hit the German
producer—hit him for no other reasons than that I
wished to believe that Noah had refused to tell the
sergeant that he was not Jewish, gaining a scar and an
end to his war in the process; that I wished to believe
that the men in Noah's family died young and that
Noah's sense of doom had some roots in reality, which
did not seem to be so, hit the innocent German producer
for no more sensible reasons than that Noah was dead
before his time, and that I had lost any place I might
have had, and the German producer was in Florence

with a woman who looked like a woman I could have been happy with.

At least for a time, which is not a small point, not *nada* since apparently what we spend in bars, clean, well-lighted, or otherwise, apparently what we spend everywhere is not money, stolen or earned, not energy, not talent, not love, but ourselves.

ASPECTS OF
THE NOVEL
BY E. M. FORSTER

a story

I put the little book down on his desk. It was hard to find a place for it; there were hundreds of loose manuscript pages, books, bound galleys, copies of *Publisher's Weekly*, letters from God knows who all squashed for an inch of space on that desk.

I noticed how gently I placed it there, even though I'd planned to rage in like a storm. Gideon did that to me; I don't know why. I didn't like that in myself, being so careful with a cripple.

"Why'd you give me that book?"

"I thought it might help."

"If you didn't think I could write the book why'd you sign it up?"

"I didn't! I signed *you* up."

He wheeled around briskly, his round face—an angel's face except for the shadow-beard that would never go away, always back by lunchtime—ignoring the pushing of those tough, stubby, chubby hands, zipping his wheelchair across the room to the window overlooking Fourth Avenue. He slammed it shut.

I jumped. Sudden noises get to me. Not that I ever saw real combat. I was always in the back streets of town making deliveries—personnel, materiel—sometimes deliveries, sometimes pick-ups—but every now and then one of those little babies would whistle by. A few of those and you stay jumpy a long time.

Gideon turned on the air-conditioning but he kept sweating. Working that wheelchair was work. Now they've got these automated ones, electronic, but Gideon's gone. I don't think he would have wanted them anyway. He liked resistance.

"Look," he said. "This is going to be one very good book and a lot of people are going to buy it. But the funny thing about a book is: somebody's got to write it. Till that happens nobody can buy it or read it."

"Pretty funny," I said. "And you think I need this little manual here, to write it?"

Gideon twisted his lips in a weird way; not a real smile and certainly not what you'd call a sneer. It was an internal smile. For all his tough act Gideon was very internal. He was talking to himself a lot when he talked to you.

"You think you can write this book because you were there? Because of all the right word-sounds—Nam, wasted, gook, whatever, because they were your natural language for three years . . ."

"Four." I loved to catch him.

"And because you *had* the experience." He ploughed ahead as if I hadn't said anything. "Because you wore that green beret."

"*Because I was there*," I said. "And you ought to know the difference by now—I was A.I.D. Agency for International Development. They just let me wear the green beret for laughs."

He looked at his watch.

"Come on," he said. "I'll buy you a drink."

Gideon knew I wasn't supposed to drink anymore. But he always pushed you to the limits. He wouldn't use an expression, "Buy you a coke," while he drank his whiskey sours. That would have been too gentle, too easy on you. It would have sent the wrong message to himself and his soul. You felt he was always sending messages to himself and his soul. Sometimes I deliberately tried to get in the way. This time I said, "You going to have one of those whiskey sours of yours?," while he struggled, alone, to get his jacket on and then swing his briefcase, heavy with manuscript, onto his lap. I hated to think what that struggle with inanimate objects might be like in the winter: scarf, gloves, overcoat, all to be gotten on with a lower body frozen stiff, forever.

"Sure," he said. "Why not?"

"That drink marks you World War II just the same as my addiction to white alcohol and what the Government likes to call "substances" marks me and my war."

He laughed and hit the sidebar of his wheelchair. "This marks my war," he said.

We went to the Cote Basque. Gideon always took us to posh places for lunch, drinks, dinner. "Small salary big expense account," he said. "That's publishing." But Cote Basque was his favorite for another reason, as well. Gideon always had at least two reasons for doing anything. But he only told you one. Sometimes he didn't tell you any. With the restaurant it was simple. They didn't want cripples in wheelchairs depressing their patrons. Once they made that clear to Gideon they had him for life. He had not been shot in the spine, flown back from Germany to endure eighteen operations, and consigned to a wheelchair, all in order to have some clown in a tux tell him where he could or could not sit in a restaurant.

He'd told me about the loud arguments with the manager—after which they were sure he'd never come back again—but there he was, round-faced, smiling, and ready to go again. Time after time. Finally, they give in. He didn't have to use talk of legal action or anything like that. He used his stubborn will. It was all he needed. They got the idea, at last, that he wasn't ever going away, wheelchair, grubby battered briefcase, and all. At the end of it they gave him a house charge account.

I was having my own taste of Gideon's will. Every time I thought a revised chapter was all set he'd come

back at me, again. I would do the changes we'd agreed
on—sometimes whether I agreed or not—and he'd take
them home and brood. Then, another round of comments in the margin of the manuscript: *needs sharpening
. . . t'aint funny . . . whose POV (point of view)? . . .
klutzy . . .* That was one of his favorites. I didn't want
to ask Gideon so I asked Kim what it meant. She'd had
an affair with a Jewish soldier in Kyoto.

"It's Yiddish," she said. "Slang. I think it means lumpy
or heavy-handed."

"That figures," I said. I never mentioned it to Gideon.

It was a tough time for me: drinking nothing but
Cokes—sometimes a dozen a day—just to have some
liquid going in and out. It was even tougher because
Kim was home a lot. She was in training to sell cosmetics. Going to college had been her first choice, but
there wasn't enough money. Disappointment made her
thirsty and she drank around the house in between
training sessions. All the while I wrestled with *Aspects
of the Novel* by this Englishman and tried to figure out
what Gideon wanted of me and what I could do to
make sure I wrote the novel that would change everything for us.

I'd started her off drinking in Tokyo where we met
when she was only nineteen. Later in San Francisco
just before I went over the edge and had to stop or die.
She thought it was fun from the start—and she was
still an innocent drinker, even when the bad reasons
started. I was always a deadly drinker; it was never
fun the way it was for Kim. For me it was salvation
or damnation. And now that I didn't do it anymore,
salvation and damnation sat on the small slabs of typewriter keys and the wheels of Gideon's metal chair.

I had been on my way back to the States to turn the
last five years or so into my fortune by writing a memoir.
And also to get my story organized on paper in case

things got ugly. But on the way back from Saigon the last time I ran into a State Department guy—a career man getting ambivalent about the war because all his wife's friends were. He was working on the Paris peace talks and he gave me a lift via special plane and via Paris. I had a week or so before I had to meet Kim's plane in New York, so I went.

I had been all the hell over Southeast Asia and in Germany before that but I'd never once put a foot in France. The State Department guy's name was Smith and he introduced me, I swear, to a guy named Jones who had this place on the Île St. Louis with an astounding view of the Seine. I was looking out at the water and wondering about things—water always makes me think about direction, looking backward or forward. Most of the time I just think about what I have to do next. It's a good way to be until it breaks down. It had broken down in Tokyo about six months before. To show you how wrecked I was, I told a lot of it to my host, who I had just met: a square, squat bullet of a man with a cigar resting in his hand.

I had told him a lot, about how I'd gotten turned in, about Kim, about the possible criminal charges, including about how I was going to write about it all. It turned out he was interested. He thought a memoir about the business side of the Vietnam War could be a good thing to tell about. It also turned out he was the Jones who wrote *From Here to Eternity*—James—and he scribbled Gideon's name and publishing house connection on a napkin.

I figured coming from a famous writer like James Jones, I would get special handling. It was special. The Gideon of those first weeks was the ideal tour of rest and recreation. He encouraged me to talk about anything at all. We made a funny pair, me strolling alongside his chair, adjusting to his pace, self-conscious. It was still a cool spring; the awful summer heat hadn't hit yet.

I did it backwards, starting with how everything had come apart, when the money stopped and you couldn't trust your sources any more—backwards all the way to my Navy time and before that to my kid sister killed in that stupid accident and how I'd wanted to be a doctor but nothing panned out. He knew more about me than Kim did.

Oh, yes, Gideon One was calming, reassuring. I looked forward to our meetings. He was like an older brother. He knew all kinds of special things like the location of tiny parks no bigger than alleys but usually having an imitation waterfall, tables with colorful umbrellas. We ate frankfurters and I admired the austere assurance with which he listened, in fact with which he lived his paralyzed wheelchair life.

It had been a while since I'd admitted to admiring another man.

The day before I signed the contract, he said, "Are you sorry about any of this. What you got into over there?"

"I guess so."

"Because if you're just pissed off at fate and other assorted government agencies the book'll have the wrong tone. There'll be no story."

"What do you think?"

"I think we've got a story."

In three weeks he was pushing me awfully hard to drop my true story in favor of doing it as a novel.

Gideon Two had arrived.

*   *   *

"**W**hy fiction?" I asked.

"Depends what you want out of this."

"I want to tell that story—the things I know about who made money out of the war and how they did it."

"You mean *you* want to make money, a lot of money."

"I want to straighten my life out. That'll take money."

"Ah, we're getting closer," Gideon said. "Do you think you're going to come to trial?"

"They're going to drop it."

"How do you know?"

"Too many people in Georgetown would be mentioned. They'll drop it."

"If there's no trial we'll do a novel."

I noted the "we'll" carefully; also the assurance with which he spoke. He was still new to me. I was used to dealing with people who had secret agendas of their own.

"**E**asy as that?" I said.

"Nobody said it was going to be easy."

He sketched the basic commercial facts of life with simple cynicism. Apparently the paperback rights— where the big money was—was usually modest for nonfiction. The big sweepstakes was in the paperback auctions for the successful novel. The book clubs also paid a lot more for novels. He could use some charm when he wanted to, old Gideon.

"You slipped into dialogue and a sketch of a scene," he said, "in your outline. It felt natural. I think you can do it. With a little help from your friends."

We were in his office, sweating and talking. It was July but Gideon always kept the air-conditioning off until you couldn't breathe one more minute. He had to tough everything out—and you with him. That was when he whizzed by me with one strong-armed twirl of the wheelchair, pulled this little book out from under the crazy jumble of papers on his desk, and tossed it at me. It was a think book, a paperback; the corners of a number of pages were turned down. I flipped through; sentences were underlined on almost every page. Then I read the title.

I noted that the book had been easily available on his desk. I was used to noting things like that, the kind of people I'd been dealing with the last five years. This was no spontaneous idea of Gideon's. I'd never had a chance. He'd decided I was going to do—"we" were going to do—a novel, all along.

"What's this?" I said. As if I didn't know.

"That's one of the friends who's going to help. There's more to writing fiction than putting 'he said' and 'she said' after lines of dialogue and adding trees." Gideon grinned; it was his cherubic grin.

"If you thought your war was tough," he said. "Just wait!" I went to the window, slammed it down, and turned on the air conditioner.

"Dammit," I said. "Why the hell do we have to sweat like this. You ought to appreciate air conditioning when you have it!" Gideon was just grinning at me. He was probably used to these little slave struggles.

The night at the Cote Basque was my moment for a big rebellion. I'd learned that damned little book by heart and it wasn't helping, it was painful. I'd gone into a kind of whirling, waking coma. A weird daytime state and sleeping badly, too; getting up all sweaty to try and write some more or reading the mysterious text. A book had not had the aura of magic for me since I'd gone to Iowa State. I would alternate reading the book and wrestling with what Gideon called my "material"—laughingly known as my life. I'd gotten a clearer vision of what I'd been doing and what it meant. It didn't always sit so nicely. I saw myself and my friends as a bunch of ordinary Americans of no special gifts, but ambitious—a typically American situation—who fell by chance into easy ways of making money on the fringes of the war.

Payoffs to contractors, kickbacks to local officials, all the paraphernalia of corruption initiated in New York, Washington, Dallas, San Francisco—the thing about such matters is, they always come down to a courier. Unlike ordinary business, *nobody puts a check in the mail.* You have to habeas corpus, as my friend Jeff Wan used to say. He meant, literally, deliver the body. Or the money, or the instructions, or, as it later developed, the substances that were as good, or better, than money.

That was where we came in. Nice, ordinary, clean-cut Americans. There was Jeff Wan, an agent for Houston Tool & Die, and his wife, Lois, who was innocent for so long, of everything except our affair.

There was Wigglesworth, the academic working in communications for A.I.D. And Phan-Phen, delicate, deferential and instantly sorry he'd gotten involved with his American friends. He'd made everyone nervous about whether he'd crack and what he'd tell.

It turned out to be Wigglesworth who cracked, earning the nickname "Wiggy" in the process. Wiggy, the least likely to go the route of guilt and religious mania—he'd been a shining star at Stamford in intellectual history before coming to Tokyo. Of course once you're outside the law you're totally dependent on honesty and friendship. And when one of you steps outside that circle everything breaks down. Wigglesworth went first and Jeff finally blew the whistle.

In the night I'd turn from memories and manuscript, imagining the phone had rung when it hadn't.

I would imagine it was a call from Wiggy in Washington—that the party was over, that there was going to be a grand jury and a trial. The call wouldn't come directly from Wiggy. An official voice would say: "Is this the residence of Lewis Griswold?" And before I could answer Wiggy would get on and tell me not to answer any questions on the phone. That he wasn't trying to get me into any trouble, but that God wanted him to tell the truth. Or I would imagine it was a call from Gideon. Both prospects scared the hell out of me.

Kim said it was the Cokes. I was drinking so many of them. She was not hip enough to be concerned about the caffeine. She said she knew an adman who worked in the Tokyo office of McCann-Erickson who worked on the Coca-Cola account and had developed an obsession. He was convinced that there was cocaine in the Coke formula. It seems the formula is a secret, still. They keep it locked up in a bank vault in Atlanta.

I didn't believe that about the Cokes. I was just drowning in the wake of that little book and my own characters, as I now thought of them. Characters: what a way to think of the people in your life! Wiggy, who might be making bad trouble for me in Washington right then—Phan-Phen, who'd died of a burst appendix, misdiagnosed accidentally or deliberately by a doctor I was pretty sure was C.I.A.; Linda Wan, who I thought I'd loved.

In the middle of my mad nights all of them were ·swimming around in some swamp, not quite the reality I remembered—and would have written about if I'd done the memoir I'd planned—and not quite what Mister E. M. Forster had in mind for me through his special agent, Gideon. Page forty-seven! *"The main facts in human life are five: birth, food, sleep, love and death."* And where does that leave pain, treachery, and madness? The kind of craziness that makes a man like Jerry Wigglesworth, who used to be a hotshot scholar in the States, go so nutty that he gets the nickname Wiggy and ends up going from office to office in Washington, begging people to listen to his story. Or the pain I gave Linda Wan and the trouble her husband, Jeff, had given me: a round robin of hurt that had no ending.

But at 4:00 one morning I saw that Forster was saying real people experience these five conditions differently than fictional characters. Characters kept on dying, he says, God knows all my dead, like my kid sister and Phan-Phen are still doing that. And that they don't care that much about food or need a normal amount of sleep but keep stewing about human relationships, if that's the way the author wants them to stew.

That sounded pretty right to me. It gave me a loony sense of freedom too, in the half-light of that tiny muggy apartment in Brooklyn Heights a few hours before the morning, to read a line like, *"If God could tell the story of the Universe, the Universe would become fictitious."*

But what seems so clear in the middle of the night can be a muddle in the morning. Maybe there *was* something in those Cokes. When I came down from my high I saw how confused I was getting between fiction and real life. And it was all a question of characters. By the time I'd re-read everything I'd written so far, allowing for a lot of struggling *not* to have a drink, a *real* drink, it was getting to be time for my afternoon appointment with Gideon. My confusion had turned into rage but it wasn't until we were sitting at the Cote

Basque, Gideon with his whiskey sour, me with my Coke, that I was able to turn it into words.

I didn't understand too much about why things had turned out the way they had. But I knew a lot about the lower and middle levels of payoffs from stateside suppliers to the military; stuff it was hard to know about unless you'd put in your time and kept alert.

I'd done both. I knew why so many companies with special government contracts had Texas addresses. And I knew which ones had dummy addresses and, in a few cases, I knew precisely why and how much money was involved in the concealment.

I had been a small player in several big games—but *I'd been a player!* Four years of my life in a game I'd lost. And what brought me back was the chance to tell about it. And now it turned out, according to Gideon, that the telling of something was not such a simple matter.

"I don't want to write a damned novel," I said. "I want to do what I came back to do."

"And what wonderful task is that?"

"Just to tell about it."

"Is that all? Well, if you recall, you came to me. The door goes both ways."

"I'm in over my head, Gideon. You and your paperback rights and book clubs . . ."

Gideon turned his hands palms up in innocence. "That's life in the big city. I didn't make the system. I'm just the messenger bringing you the news."

My anger drained down. He could always do that to me, take the edge off. "I never even read novels much. And now, writing one . . . I don't know . . ."

As if he could sniff my anger melting he said, "The first three chapters are terrific. Needs a little polishing, that's all."

"I know your polishing," I said.

"Well," Gideon waved his hand as if I'd expressed some trivial complaint. "Nothing comes quick," he said, "except bad, unexpected accidents. You're on your way. That's what counts."

I lightened up. "The odd thing is—I *am* getting into it. I don't have any big ideas about Art like E. M. . . ."

"Edward Morgan," Gideon said. "He made me break my rule. Never trust a writer who uses two initials.

"I've been reading him in the wee hours of Brooklyn Heights." I reached to hold onto feeling angry. "This crap about flat and round characters . . ."

"Page sixty-seven."

"Big deal. So you've done this steamroller act before, with some other poor bastard, and you know the textbooks by heart . . ."

That was Gideon's cue to change. Instantly he charmed and disarmed. With that same disheveled smile he sang sweet songs of writers with far less experience—hell, writers barely deserving of the name, with *no* experience—and how he'd nurtured their manuscripts from doubting disasters to bestsellers.

"We're not talking," he said, fishing the fruit salad from his drink and placing it on the saucer, "about making you an artist: no slim symbolic volume by L. W. Griswold. We're talking about plain old Lewis Griswold developing enough craft to make a readable novel—so you can move and entertain the people who read your book while you're giving them the information that only you can give. Got it?"

I got it all right. It sounded like a speech he'd made before to other hungry, angry amateurs who had to be kept in line.

I also noted the absence of the "we." That sounded like progress. I stirred the lime in my coke. The fruit salad in my drink was essential to give the illusion of a mixed drink.

"A lot of the stuff you say and Edward Morgan says makes sense in the middle of the night in Brooklyn Heights—but in the morning it turns to crap in the typewriter."

"How do you like Brooklyn Heights? A little tame after the Far East?"

"Listen, we're grateful to have a place to stay while I'm hanging by my thumbs." A surprise advantage. The threat of gratitude terrified him.

"Any time," he said, waving an impatient hand. "A very small deal. Just don't pee on the floor. My Uncle Alfred is very particular about who pees on his floor."

The threat of sentiment had been averted. Gideon felt safe again. But just to hold onto his lead he pulled the first three chapters of my manuscript out of his briefcase. It was always right there on his lap—if you live in a wheelchair the lap becomes a kind of catch-all.

The margins on the pages were thick with scrawls.

"Just a little polishing," I said. If a voice could be pale I thought my voice sounded pale.

"Easy, buddy, you wanted to know about flat and round characters."

"I said I thought it was bullshit. I didn't say I wanted to know."

"Same thing," he said, implacable. "Your guy is flat where he should be round and Lois Wan—she's good—but she's too complicated—round when she should be—well, you get the idea. Here . . ." He hunched over the manuscript on the table.

I sat frozen. It was the moment to pull out. I was broke and I could be in deeper trouble than I knew about. *But the one thing I had left was what had happened to me. I had done what I'd done and seen what I'd seen. There was a certain solidness in that. Maybe* you couldn't buy food with it but it felt as if you could stand on it.

He was damned smart, old Gideon Two; he knew what was going on. He leaned back a second and said, "You don't have to keep on. You can call it off, pay back the advance, and maybe somebody else'll give you a contract to do it your way. Anything's possible."

I called out, "Waiter, Stoly on the rocks."

The damn fool waiter almost ruined my gesture.

"Sir?" he asked.

I said, very carefully, "Stolichnaya vodka. With ice, please."

I didn't wait for a reaction. I said: "Her name in the story is not Lois Wan. I forgot to change to the fictional name from the first draft."

"At this stage," he said, "names don't count." He waited while the waiter put the cold vodka in front of me.

"How about nicknames," I said. "Like Stoly, for example?"

I have to give him the credit. He didn't take a beat. He was not about to notice my monumental gesture. His finger jabbed at the pages and he hunched over again. I was implacable, now. "I don't understand what that stuff means. About flat characters being 'humorous.' "

"It doesn't mean funny," he said.

The wheelchair shot back from the table. "Come on, old buddy," he said. "Let's have some dinner."

I grinned. We hadn't talked about having dinner, tonight. I figured I'd caught his attention. If not his concern.

"I'll bring my drink," I said.

He ordered the worst food possible for a man who could never exercise anything but his arms: a monster steak, fried potatoes, that kind of thing. Lots of butter on the bread. I ordered another Stoly and poked at a piece of swordfish without much interest. Whenever I drank, food lost its sex appeal.

Gideon ate and talked; how he talked. He talked about adding dimension to my hero and taking it away from my heroine. He told me the "flat" characters didn't have to be thin—just one-dimensional. When I told him Kim's theory about Coca-Cola and cocaine, he said to give that obsession to my heroine.

"Nothing like a few obsessions to make a character jump off the page," he said. "And it's about Coca-Cola which conquered the Far East long before the U.S. Army arrived. A double-whammy is always the best." He kept talking. He would talk about everything, apparently, except the fact that I was drinking again. By the time the meal was over his steak was gone, my fish was cold, and I was bombed.

I had the courage I needed to attack.

"Listen, I've been over those chapters twice."

"Go over them again. And start the next one."

"I'm going to do this the way I want!"

"Anyway you like, old buddy. You're the one who's on the spot."

"My God, your clock stopped in the army. You still talk PX talk. Civilians don't have buddies."

His hand was up again, high, signaling for the check. It was one of the swift gestures I remembered from my drinking days. It means the owner of the hand saw trouble coming and was calling a halt.

It felt familiar and good. I'd gotten a measure of control back. He was signing the check when I got one of those daring notions I used to enjoy when I was drinking. I took the E. M. Forster book and shoved it towards him.

"Here," I said. "I'm through with this. Enough." My gesture of independence lasted about one second.

Gideon grabbed the little paperback, opened it and tore it in half and as far down as the remaining pages would tear. It was a shocking thing to see—a book being destroyed—I don't quite know why. It wasn't the only copy in the world or anything, but the sound it made was unnatural. Nobody tears books up. You don't even throw them away when you're finished; you donate them to hospitals or the army or somewhere. They're meant to be permanent. It was a disgusting thing to see.

There was a stir at the tables around us. Gideon threw the debris onto the table; some of the pages floated to the floor. The headwaiter watched us from the front of the dining room and behind him, the manager. Something told me they'd won their battle. This would be Gideon's last visit to the Cote Basque. There would be no more disabled editors to depress the patrons.

"Why the hell'd you do that?" I said.

"I hate to hem in a free spirit, like you. You can make your characters rectangular for all I give a damn."

He shoved the wheelchair back from the table, executed a swift turn, and headed for the exit. I followed. I had no choice. A lot of heads stared straight in front of them while their eyes followed us out. A dynamic duo: shouting, tearing up books, wheelchairs.

Out on the sidewalk it was like walking in a warm soup. I began to sweat right away. Gideon's car was parked half a block away. It was one of those special cars you could operate without using your feet, all hand controls. It was a Chevy. I never dreamed Chevy would bother to make special vehicles for the disabled.

In minutes he had wheeled himself to the car, unlocked the door, hoisted himself onto the front seat, and collapsed the chair in one practiced movement. The exertion must have been awful for a man of his bulk but he did not make a murmur. He paused and seemed stuck for an instant. I forgot the Gideon rule

of never helping. But in moving towards him I tripped
on a sidewalk crack. He pointed a finger at me.

"I'll give you a perfect flat character," he said. "A
drunk. Predictable, comical in spite of himself—stum-
bles on cue . . . can be visualized by the reader in one
sentence. 'Lewis Griswold, in the course of an evening's
drinking would become jocose, bellicose, morose, lach-
rymose, and, finally, comatose.' "

Once, during a poker game in the army barracks at
Fort Meade, Maryland, some young tough convinced
himself that I was cheating—I wasn't—and threw a
glass of vodka in my face. That's the way Gideon's
speech made me feel. For a minute I had no breath to
talk with. I could hear myself breathe but I couldn't
use my voice. I had finally bloodied the kid's upper lip
pretty bad. But I couldn't do anything now. Gideon
waited.

"Aren't you ever afraid," I said. At last I was able to
say something. "That you might go too far?"

"What's too far?"

"That you could push somebody like me—over the
top. That you could make me feel like such a piece of
shit that I might keep on drinking—" I felt a surge of
sorrow as I spoke. It disgusted me, but I couldn't do
anything about it. "And I might kick off for good."

"And it would be my fault. Right?"

"Right. And I can't hit you, right? You can't hit a
cripple, even if he's trying to do you in, right?"

"Wrong," he said flat out.

I stared at him in the dark. The car embraced him
from behind; the half-folded wheelchair was like a weird
metal and leather lectern or pulpit. His eyes gave back
my stare; icy blue they were.

"What makes you so different from the rest of us
poor struggling folks?"

Gideon gave the locked wheels of his chair a little shake. *"Because I could be selling pencils in this thing,"* he said. *"One ounce of pity and you're a fair mark for pencils."*

One of us, probably me, must have been talking pretty loud because a couple of women had stopped nearby and were watching, one of them fanning herself with a program of some kind. They were wondering, I suppose, if the drunk was going to actually attack this guy in the wheelchair.

In my vodka haze I reached for words. Some people become eloquent when they're stoned; I get dumber and dumber. I'm too desperate; the mark of a deadly drinker. I wasn't looking for words, anyway; I was searching for a wound to poke at.

"How come you got shot in the back?" I said. "In the spine. Were you facing the wrong way?"

The two women walked by us in that elegant upper East Side darkness. I guess I'd lowered my voice and the danger of murder had clearly passed.

"It was an accidental American bullet," Gideon said. "A buddy of mine, actually."

"Everybody's got a buddy."

"Yeah, I was ahead of my time. Happened all the time in your war. Only not by accident."

"Some buddy."

Gideon collapsed the chair completely with a series of metallic clanks, like chains. He swung, a special kind of discus thrower, turning from the waist, and hurled it into the seat next to him.

"You don't know anything," he said. "The guy who did it loved me. A buddy of buddies. It killed him when it happened."

"I'll bet."

"You'd lose! I could trust him, today, more than your

Washington friends—the ones you're waiting on to see if you go to trial or not."

I leaned against the hot metal of the car, as exhausted as if it were the morning after. My high was gone.

"You're flat, Gideon," I said. "In one sentence: 'Gideon, wounded in action, stuck helplessly in a wheelchair for life, decided to take aggressive action on every front, always, so no one could ever feel pity for him.' "

Gideon grinned. I saw his teeth, pumpkin-like, in the dark.

"Close," he said. He grabbed his right leg with two pudgy hands and swung it up and under the dashboard and then did it again with the left leg.

"Close, but no cigar." He turned the ignition key. "Go home and get it right," he said and tossed the envelope holding my manuscript at me.

I went home drunk and defeated. Kim was very quiet the next day. I took in nothing for two days but black coffee and Cokes. Then I circled the typewriter for a day and sat down in a kind of trance and finished the draft of the novel in fifteen weeks. It was either a sustained act of rebellion or submission; but it had as much to do with Gideon as it did with the "characters" in my story. The first change I made was to put the Wiggy character into a wheelchair. I'd seen a lot of the wounded taking R & R and I knew how to do that. It went smooth as cream after that. Well, not that smooth. In fact it was hell some days. But at least I was able to put one word in front of another and each scene seemed to lead forward. Oh, I gave Lois Wan—Sara Hsu as I named her—the Coca-Cola/cocaine obsession Gideon had suggested. I stayed away from him. The notes in the margin were conversation enough.

I'd gone out and bought a copy of *Aspects of the Novel* by E. M. Forster which Gideon had torn up in that spectacular way. It was comforting to know that it was there in the store and I could buy one. I took it home sort of amused at myself for thinking of it as a friend. Now that Gideon had turned against it in a weird way, my resistance to it was gone.

I read the part about plot; about how "The King died" and then the Queen died was a story but "The King died and then the Queen died of grief" was a plot. It was a real help to me and I was grateful and learning about gratitude at the same time.

Six weeks into my marathon a letter came from the publisher. Except it was marked Please Forward and it was from Wiggy. When you cut through all the crazy talk about God punishing us all and Sin and Hell, what it said was: I could expect a phone call in a few weeks. People had believed him at last and a grand jury would be called and some wonderful human being he'd met, who happened to be an assistant D.A., would be getting in touch with me. There was one small touch of the old Wigglesworth. He said he knew I was trying to hide out—but that the kind of people now "on the case," as he put it, would have no trouble finding me or my phone number. Just like the good old days.

I always knew I'd hear. Not how or when—or even from who. But I always knew there would be some kind of a trial, that I was just getting extra good at kidding myself that it would all go away. I wondered if Gideon always knew also.

I remembered him saying, "If there's no trial we'll do a novel."

It was too late to change now. The phone call would undoubtedly come and the grand jury summons would come after that. In the meantime I would finish my novel—as I now thought of it without shame—collect the second half of my advance, get an apartment for Kim and me, and find a lawyer. The book and the inevitable trial together conspired to give me the shape of a life. I didn't tell Gideon about the letter or the promised phone call from Washington. That could come later.

Later got to be very important. Later on I would attend to Kim and her daytime Scotches and her dumb training for a dumb job. Everything could come later, after I'd finished. After I saw the look on Gideon's face I wanted to see, everything else could begin.

Gideon died on the Wednesday after Labor Day. He was knocked on his back by a heart attack. I read it in the *Times*. He'd had the heart attack at home then—bang—pneumonia—and out! I'd turned in the finished manuscript ten days before; left it at his office not wanting to face him until he had read it.

The obit said there was to be no service, just a private cremation ceremony for the family. I didn't know his family. But I figured Uncle Alfred would be calling and it was time to start packing up.

Two days later the manuscript came back in the mail. When I saw the thick scribbles in the margins I suddenly got the idea that I would never see Gideon again. I mean it stopped being an idea at that moment. Old Gideon, so scared people might feel sorry for him. At least he'd gotten hurt in the right war. He wasn't a back-alley courier picking up an easy dollar in the shadows. He was right inside the center: a hero-on-the-hoof, in maybe the last war everybody agreed somebody had to fight. It might not carry the day or the night, at 4:00 A.M. in a bed with legs that couldn't move. But it must have been worth *something*, a guy like him, to carry a wound that nobody could laugh at, or put down, or say boo to, somebody as proud as him.

I sure as hell wouldn't want to be crippled, but it might be nice to be proud. Then I got teary and felt foolish and scared for myself, too.

"Well," I told Kim, "he can't stop me feeling sorry for him now."

She was packing the few special things she cared about; rolling the breakables up in newspaper; a porcelain Hindu dancer; a bud vase. I told her that because she might have seen my reaction. But she just kept carefully placing those little packages into a carton. We were sitting in the kitchen, the manuscript on the kitchen table.

Finally she said something. "Couldn't we go back?" she said. "He wasn't so nice to you, anyway."

"Even if we could go back—what would I do?"

My mind was running. I'd always been good at business. If you call what I'd been doing out there business. It wasn't exactly buying low and selling high. It was who needed what you had badly enough. Like me and Gideon. I needed what he knew—he and Mister Forster. We'd done our work, finished now. And I was spoiled for the old business, uncertain in the new.

The one thing I hadn't done since Gideon died was to go over the pages and see what he'd scrawled. There would be somebody else to deal with at the publishers. It was so hard to figure—he went everywhere comfortable, trapped for life in a wheelchair, from which, if you allowed an ounce of pity you'd be selling pencils on a street corner, but at home in his skin. Me, my nerves scramble on my bones when I have to talk to strangers or any new people these days. Him in his chair; Mister round character. He was round all right.

I told as much of this to Kim as I could make her understand. She surprised me.

"You've been tossed around the world too much, Lew," she said. "It takes a thing from you. He was stuck right in his place, in his chair. But it was his place. A chair is a place."

Sometimes I couldn't tell if it was the Scotch talking or if there were still things I had to learn about Kim. The oriental women I've known try to look like flat characters. But it's just a way of looking, not the way they are.

I squeezed a half a lime into my Coke and went to the kitchen table to leaf through the pages on the kitchen table. In the margins Gideon had scrawled his signatures: *Weak from paragraph two on . . . No guts . . . rewrite from the gut . . . falls apart in the middle of the scene . . . No balls . . .*

What energy the dead could muster! What aggression from the crematory fires! It should have been no surprise to me. Half of the people dragging me to a criminal trial were dead. I finished my Coke and tentatively, very slowly, Kim said to me, "You want to have a drink?"

I looked at her as if I was testing her. "You mean one of these—or a real drink?"

She turned those brownish-black eyes away; couldn't face me. "Whatever you want," she said.

I sat facing the open window. To look out I had to see the pile of manuscript on the kitchen table, with the black marks all along the white sides of the paper. It looked like I wasn't finished yet. I felt the rise of the old frustration and rage: whenever you thought you were finished with Gideon he came back at you, and you had to start all over again. It was endless.

I got up and looked at the pages more closely. I stared, trancelike; everything felt mixed together, Gideon being gone along with all the other losses, Phan-Phen, my kid sister, the confusion of those years which had seemed so lively and practical, while things held together: picking up from Jeff, delivering—everybody always glad to see me arrive and then R&R until the next time—the strange isolation of my affair with Linda Wan . . . "It's always oriental women with you because you think your own kind are critical of you while others are just grateful." Wiggy's pronouncement just before the break . . . an amateur psychologist before becoming an amateur prophet.

I'd never thought much about the future, never thought I could parlay the small-time stuff I was moving around into some big hit, never even thought I'd get Lois Wan to leave Jeff and marry me. In fact, I realized now, looking at a story I seemed to have written, with a beginning, a middle, and end, that I'd never made any planned connections. It had all been so heedless until Gideon. Blind alleys of days and nights, mixed motives, missed chances, a jig-saw puzzle with a few key pieces always left out.

But this was different. I began to get excited as I riffled through the pages. The comments didn't trouble me so much now. In fact they got my adrenalin going. I would insert Wiggy's letter there, right there, to give a stronger spine to the scene. And that remark about feeling safer with oriental women—that could be said by another character for a grittier conflict.

It was as if I saw the chaotic stream of my days and nights through the eyes of some super-Gideon; some giant cloud-face of an editor, like a special effect in a movie; a cheap, cinematic point, the great editor-in-the-sky shaping the drunken progression of dumb experiences into some sense: beginning, middle, yes even maybe an ending.

Nothing was exempt. Even the cold commercialization of it all into a would-be bestseller—I saw that Gideon insult, which had so pissed me off, as a perverse act of faith; a weird conferring of grace as only that imprisoned, imprisoning wonderful son-of-a-bitch could confer.

It extended much further than just putting an okay stamp on my haphazard career on the fringes of that war—the war which had made a lot of people sick, some mad, some dead, and some rich. It went all the way back to the sense I'd always had, but never admitted, that my kid sister had died instead of me; that it was my fault. It was a stupid car accident, so I know it's a wild idea. I mean she was crossing the street and I was downtown in school. But you can't know a thought is crazy until you put it in place, admit it, and hook it up to other thoughts, other places and people.

My mother calling it a judgment of God—as if it made the senseless smash-up of a little life more acceptable, if you brought God into it. I hated the idea, God judging seven-year-old kids. I knew she meant my father and his women at the factory, but that was just as sickening. Any way you took the death of my kid sister as anything but random was awful.

Strangely, it was Gideon's surprise dying that seemed to put all of these things into some ranking. The way he'd insisted on putting the gains and losses of what happened to me in the Far East into some order—all the deaths and betrayals organized into fictional order: the events moving forward, the characters flat or round. His being dead made it possible to feel things settled. That was an unpleasant notion. My mother had my sister settled into heaven. But Gideon's dying and poking at me and my manuscript, now that I could no longer poke back, was urgent, continuing.

In a feverish scribble I began to jot down items.

- The impossible accident of making love to Lois Wan in the American Embassy, when anyone could have walked through the doors and discovered us.

- Finding myself seated opposite Gideon's wheelchair and realizing how important it was to me to please him.
- The very first day Jeff asked me if I would drop off a package at a bar near the harbor and would I please not ask him what was in it.

I was breathless in the rush of connections, of backward and forward movement. I muttered, "Gideon, Gideon . . ." like a prayer of gratitude.

The feeling of shape, of cause and effect, was like a thrill in my blood.

"Hey, the King died and then the Queen died of grief," I said and laughed and felt giddy.

But Kim didn't hear me because she was going into the living room to answer the phone.

BROOKSMITH
BY HENRY JAMES

a story

for Muriel Shine

98

Celia Morris met Zoe Lee her first week on campus. Zoe was tall, aggressively shy, with striking shiny black skin and cheekbones set high and angry. She was not beautiful, only large and austere; not gifted as a student, only desperately persistent. Celia was afraid of her for some reason and played with the idea of screening her out of the class. In the end she didn't have the nerve.

Everything scared Celia, her husband's death sitting on her so recent and so heavy. Michael Morris's death was one of those losses which strike whole communities. It hit me hard and I came into his orbit late in his career and life. It hit all of us—the designers, the writers, directors, the painters, an actor—such as myself—who relied on Michael Morris for more than just professional financial advice. We received from him what I can only call grace: a humane address to the crazy, crushing world of theater and writing and art. If we were so badly struck down, how much more would Celia be wiped out. We watched and waited.

Celia couldn't afford to wait. In his caring so eloquently and elegantly for all of us, Michael had not taken care to become rich or even mildly plush. I think that since we all assumed he would always be there for us, he picked up on the loony idea of his own immortality. It was typical of him. The security of the people who made the beautiful things he admired so much was more important than his own. So his financial wit died with him. And Celia, the wife of the attorney-at-law to the arts, inherited the fate more common to the widows of artists and scientists: she was broke. Still dazed by what had happened to her she had to go back to teaching college English at the City University.

Now all this was in the rough-and-tough days of the sixties in New York. Campuses were crowded, issues flamed on every walk and lawn; the placard and the bullhorn were as basic as books. Through the whirling chaos Celia walked, oblivious. Everyone's personal history must intersect with the general condition. And if one is more intense, the other gives way. Before the grief of losing Michael Morris, those dramatic campus events gave way. Celia was a ghost haunted by ghosts.

Still there was registration. Nothing is as real as registration. And nothing rouses the half-dead as well as a roiling group of students raising questions about a class you've only half thought through. With relief Celia realized she could still do it. She talked about the need for all kinds of literature, relevant (and irrelevant? she wondered) as well as more distantly applied fictions. She seized on two Jameses, James Baldwin and Henry James.

This done, she divided the class along voluntary lines—it was the fashion of the hour—and the blacks and Puerto Ricans clustered into one group, the lower middle class and a smattering of middle-class whites in the second. When the session ended, Zoe Lee towered over her, a shadow cutting off her light. She was the first to hand in her paper. Thanks for nothing, Celia thought, staring down the sullen young woman. This is a first for me, Celia thought, hating a student. And one who's done nothing to me. Grief makes you crazy, she decided.

It made her drunk that night in a half-hour flat. She sat on the carpet in the living room, shoes kicked off, dinner-less, glass in hand, and tried to read papers. But the room was full of echoes, distractions. In the corner the piano sang silently, sang the Schubert G Major Sonata which Paul Badura-Skoda had played twenty years earlier. (The pianist had been grateful—saved by Michael's skill from what he'd called his financial death wish.) It became the family joke—all these gifted men and women saved from financial suicides by Michael Morris, a roly-poly British lawyer who loved the artist and the arts so deeply he could see no difference between them. And they loved him back, making his home an oasis of song, poetry, and general conversation which even that confused time recognized as extraordinary.

Celia built a fire and crowded out music, laughter; all the delicious debris of the past by reading papers. Zoe Lee's paper jumped out at her. It was awful! The term "broken English," usually reserved for foreigners, came to her mind. "Writing means to have a thing in which you be told what things mean in the world . . ."

God, she thought, this class is going to be murder. She rambled through the two Jameses and chose two stories: "Sonny's Blues" by James Baldwin and "Brooksmith" by Henry. She would not blaze trails. She would act out the cliché. The blacks get Baldwin, the whites get James. No illusions with either group. "Sonny's Blues" was an elegiac tale of a gifted black man and his troubled younger brother who, finally, he could not save. "Brooksmith" was the tale of a butler at one of those Jamesian salons of the imagination, so spoiled by the quality of the discourse at his master's evenings that he cannot survive the man's death and all that vanishes with it.

Some sane, still sober part of Celia knew she was attracted by the echo of her life with Michael. Brooksmith, like dear, round, appreciative Michael, was an artist without an art, attending those who owned and exercised the gifts. These days any echo would do. She took it and fell asleep on the floor in a blur of books.

The next day she zombied through both sections of the class, assigning the stories and trying not to look at Zoe Lee who, in any case, turned out to be absent.

After lunch she was almost knocked down in the hallway by Zoe Lee.

"What . . . what is it?"

"I couldn't get to class." Her famous icy aplomb was gone. "What was the assignment?"

Celia told her and watched the tall ghost flee towards the exit.

C wonders what Z has on her that shakes her up so. They're as far apart in lives as in the alphabet—though Celia knows nothing of Zoe's life. She sleeps badly that night and doses heavily with coffee the next day. She writes the assignment briskly on the blackboard:

SONNY'S BLUES BY JAMES BALDWIN Write eight hundred words on theme, et cetera, et cetera . . .

A hand shoots up instantly. Celia's fears confirmed. It is, of course, Zoe.

"What is it, Miss Lee."

"But you say "Brooksmith" by Henry James."

"I said—what?"

"When I asked you in the hall . . ."

Celia is shaken. What a dumb mistake. I am going crazy, she thought. I have to get away. I started working

too soon after death. Black is the color of mourning
. . . Z is the last letter of the alphabet.

You need more time, she tells herself.

To Zoe Lee she said, "All right," trying to sound
professorially certain. "Have you read 'Brooksmith'?"

"Yes, I have."

"Then you do the James."

Amazement arrives that night. It is the not vodkas and
the heavyweight wine which overwhelm her light-
weight tuna fish dinner and leave her lightheaded. It
is not a phantasm. It is the fact that the only paper on
any topic that was worth a damn was Zoe Lee on
"Brooksmith." Passionate, intelligent, infused with an
offbeat but central understanding of the tale, even the
awful locutions could not destroy it, could not wipe out
Celia's sense of discovering something, someone.

*"Brooksmith be spoiled by being only part way into
the beautiful world of his master Mister Offard. It can
be a curse on you, they let you in part way so you can't
go back and they hate for you to go forward."*

"This is a very good paper."

"Good," Zoe Lee said. Ice! But Celia was hot on the
trail.

"It's so much better than the first one. Why?"

"The first was just to talk smart so I could get into
the class."

"What's your direction, Zoe?"

"What?"

"What do you want to do?"

"A nurse. I have to be a nurse."

"I see. But still, it's so unusual to do such a good paper out of the blue. James is not an easy writer."

"I don't care about your writers," Zoe Lee said. "I never heard his damn name before you." Her eyes burned with the blind intensity that had been scaring the hell out of Celia. "I am Brooksmith," she said.

And it all poured out. She lived with her mother and three sisters in Bedford Stuyvesant. They were all prostitutes. Her sisters thought she was crazy for wanting a different life. Her mother was in a rage against her, hoping she would fail.

"I ain't going to do it and keep on doin' it for no man I don't know and just wants my ass—and get beat up like my sister Adelia so she have a hurt in her kidney all the time after. I am going to be a nurse."

And she told Celia how she felt spoiled, like Brooksmith. She had no real place any more but she didn't want to be left behind like him, to die. Astonishing Celia again, she wept. When the white woman tried to touch her hand in confusion and consolation, Zoe Lee stood and towered over her.

"You'll be able to do it," Celia said. "Why shouldn't you?" She could hear the ring of nothingness in her voice. So could Zoe Lee.

"Who the hell are you here," she said. The contempt that rang in her voice may have been precisely what Celia had feared all along, who knows?

"It's not your damned class. I can't hardly do the science class. They the ones I need for the nursing. What the damned shit you know about it!"

"I didn't say I know . . ."

"Everything come easy to you . . ."

"That's not true."

Celia is hurt and feels, at the same time, foolishly formal. She takes a breath and can hardly believe what she is confiding.

"I'm having a terrible time and you know nothing about it."

"I know your man is dead. Whole class knows that . . ."

Celia is ready to give up. "That's not your business." Control returns. "I will try to help you. I want to help."

"Yeah—" Zoe wipes her eyes with a tissue.

Celia can handle no more of this insane unwarranted intimacy. It's already more than she's counted on. She was up to a quick compromise, no more. She feels sweaty, exhausted.

"Then perhaps," she says, "we understand each other—and we can go on from here."

But going on is always more difficult than it seems. Celia was determined to do the right thing by this extraordinary young woman. We've been spoiled, she thought. We've both of us been spoiled. She'd arranged a science tutor for Zoe, had given her a good grade in the literature seminar, and, at the last, lost track of her; as one does, finally, of just about all students, even those who raise questions about one's own life.

Four years after her first encounter with Zoe, Celia entered the hospital for an operation, nature uncertain. I had called her for reasons of my own; my acting life was drying up to a point I could no longer afford to ignore. I was playing with the idea of teaching drama at a university until a summer stock job came through, and I wanted Celia's advice.

When the department secretary told me of her illness I went to visit her. We had not been close for a long time. But I still thought about the old days—the perfect evenings—when Michael was alive. Since he'd died, things had not been the same for me either, not only socially but financially. In fact a lawyer and an accountant had helped get me into precisely the kind of mess Michael was so exquisitely adept at keeping me out of. So, as Freud says of dreams, my visit was overdetermined.

I found Celia quite excited. "Listen" she said, "There's a student of mine here. I just saw her. My God, you can't imagine . . ."

"Oh?" The room was empty.

"Across the hall."

"Is it serious?"

"She's a nurse."

And she told me, lying there in her flowered nightgown, the story of Zoe Lee; just the way I've told it here. Then she led me on a foray to find her. Zoe was, as advertised, tall, strikingly midnight-black, and austere. She was making some entries on a chart and looked up at us.

"Hello, Zoe," Celia said.

She looked down at us, coolly. "You know me, Ma'am?" The "Ma'am" must have been an acquired piece of post-nursing-school politesse. "How do you know my name?"

"You were my student."

"What class was that?"

"English. Your first year. Don't you remember? You wrote that wonderful paper." Celia was shaky on my arm; I could feel her rigid, trembling. "It was on a story by Henry James—"Brooksmith." And you told me—" I wanted to stop Celia but there was no way.

"You said—" Celia raised her voice in proud imitation, "*I am Brooksmith!*" The phrase hung in the air for a moment.

At last Zoe Lee allowed herself a small smile. It lit up nothing.

"I remember you. You're Mrs. Morris."

"Yes," Celia said. "I see you've done what you set out to do. You're a nurse."

Zoe permitted herself a nod. "But I never said anything about any Brooksmith. I don't know that name."

"Brooksmith . . .?"

"I remember your class. We read James Baldwin. 'Sonny's Song', some title like that."

" 'Sonny's Blues'."

"That's right. Well, I have patients to tend."

And she was gone. Celia was inconsolable. I saw, too, that she was sicker than I'd let myself notice. She was weak, one eye half-closed. In the next half-hour she reviewed everything: Zoe Lee, her lost Michael, their life together, then Zoe all over again, on some endless loop of memory.

"How could she have forgotten?"

"It was only a story assignment to her," I said stupidly.

"Oh, no," Celia said. "You don't understand."

Celia was stuck in the hospital for a long course of treatment. But she made some phone calls for me and during the next few weeks, with her help, I began to mend my frayed life by working as a substitute teacher of drama. Not being a true academic I found myself with a certain unconventional freedom. And, for some perverse reason, I read "Brooksmith"—the little story which had caused such an upheaval in Celia's sense of things. And, still more perversely, I assigned it to my class. *Write five hundred words on the central dramatic conflict . . .*

More important, I felt a kind of intimate acquaintance with the taciturn British servant. Being exiled myself from my theatrical past—a past which had shed its glamor long ago, but which I still missed—I could un-

derstand him. I suppose I felt spoiled in my own way.
I'd had my moments. The *Times* reviewer once said I
had a certain grace. And I'd played in Pinter at the
Royal Shakespeare a long time ago, and Pinter himself
had said I was "strong." And here I was teaching drama
to students whose idea of tragedy was the violent death
of rock stars. To push myself on, I plunged into it with
a high seriousness, research and all. And made an
interesting discovery. I found the buried roots of
"Brooksmith."

EXCERPT FROM THE NOTEBOOKS OF HENRY JAMES
Another little thing was told me the other day about
Mrs. Duncan Stewart's lady's maid, Past, who was with
her for years before her death and whom I often saw
there. She had to find a new place of course, on Mrs.
S's death, to relapse into ordinary service. Her sorrow,
the way she felt the change and the way she expressed
it . . .
    *"Ah, yes ma'am, you have lost your mother, and it's
a great grief, but what is your loss to mine? You continue
to live with clever, cultivated people; but I fall again
into my own class. I shall never see such company—
hear such talk—again. She was so good to me that I
lived with her, as it were; and nothing will ever make
up to me for the loss of her conversation. Common,
vulgar people now; that's my lot for the future.*

I read this late one night, wonderfully struck by the
possibilities of transformation. So Brooksmith had been
something, someone, before becoming a perfect but
spoiled butler in the perfect salon. He had been a lady's

maid named Past, with a sensibility above her station. Then why not a Brooklyn black trying to escape the prostitute's fate? And who could know what he'd be the next time?

I felt oddly excited. I was not too played out, too lost, to be beyond discovering something. I'd unearthed some sort of permanent patron saint of aristocratic nostalgia. The morning couldn't come soon enough. I was eager to share my find with Celia. But when I got to the hospital I found she'd taken a turn for danger in her illness.

She could not register who was visiting her and her fever was high. I hesitated at the door; an oxygen tent inhaled and exhaled. A black form shook a thermometer, cranked the bed. The next time I came, early the following evening, Zoe Lee was still hovering over Celia, as if she were caring for a mother.

I asked the head nurse at the station about it, as indirectly as I could.

"Ah, Zoe and Mrs. Morris," she said. "Zoe's pulling her through. Every day a little more, a little better."

"Really . . ."

"Well, they were old friends, it seems," the head nurse said. "Zoe asked to be put on her case when she heard about Mrs. Morris's condition. And Zoe is in great demand; everyone has an eye on that young woman. She's special, Zoe is. Self-educated, too. Extraordinary."

"Yes," I said. "So I see."

THE PSYCHOPATHOLOGY
OF EVERYDAY LIFE
BY SIGMUND FREUD

a story

In Volume II of the Ernest Jones biography of Sigmund Freud, Jones notes, regarding Freud's discovery of the pressure on the conscious mind to repress—what the rest of us call forgetting:

The Psychopathology of Everyday Life, 1904. Its main theme—the influence of unconscious processes in interfering with conscious functioning—was sharply criticized at first by psychologists, but has been more widely accepted and generally known than any other of Freud's teachings. The phenomena in question have since been given the name of "parapraxes." (Literally False Practice.)

Can you imagine how it might have turned out if Katherine Eudemie had forgotten her child in the coat room of The Russian Rendezvous in March instead of a glorious, sunny June? Think of the women's coats soggy with snow—the men's trench coats soaked with wet—the little girl, Tulip, under a curse of endless sniffles. Impossible to think of raising a child in such an environment.

Also, in June the business slows down, but somebody is always on duty in the coat room for the occasional rainy day, the umbrellas like sentinels in the stand in front of the revolving door. There were two people on duty. Usually one of the Old Guard regulars, round, soft, sixty-five-ish or more—like Sasha, who fled Russia to America via Paris with the Chauve Souris company as a young girl in the twenties. And there was always someone like Myrna.

Myrna was one of the "going-to-be's" for which the RR was well known. You know, going to be an actress, going to be a writer, going to be a dancer. They were usually young, but perhaps not all that different from the stylish types ordering blini with red caviar, or karsky shashlik, inside the dining room.

"Going-to-be" is a long process. Especially when it comes to writing and music, acting and dancing. In those sacred spheres exactly what and where one has arrived at is uncertain. The dining room of the RR was full of men and women circling each other in the endless dance of confirmation; moths whose success could only be confirmed by direct contact with the flame. Sometimes the main difference between the people caring

for the coats and hats and those checking them were
the burn marks.

It all began with Katherine Eudemie forgetting a book:
The Psychopathology of Everyday Life by Sigmund Freud.
It was not the kind of book Katherine usually read. But
exhausted by the impossible task of getting a second
novel published she had secretly decided to become a
psychotherapist.

This was after years of ferocious dedication as a
patient. Her embarrassment at the status of being a
permanent basket-case led her to joke with friends:
"When I was a kid in Chicago I never played Doctor.
I always knew I'd grow up to be a patient." But that
wore thin after a while: she was getting to be too
familiar. To survive in Russian Rendezvous New York
you must never be pigeonholed. Once they put you in,
it's almost impossible to fly out again.

You must either constantly succeed or constantly
surprise. Katherine had succeeded once, as the beautiful
young provincial, a philo-Judaic writer with a "sound"
as the reviews put it. But the sound increasingly became
a whine. When her suicide attempts no longer attracted
the appropriate attention she had a baby.

Everyone took babies seriously!

Her sound changed.

"Having Tulip puts life into perspective," she told
her agent at an RR lunch.

"How old is she now?"

"Four next month."

"God, where do the years go?"

Where? Eight since Katherine's first novel was published, six since she'd married the editor-anthologist
Jackson Eudemie, and two weeks since she'd decided

to become a therapist. A failed actress friend had done it. It didn't take years to accomplish any more, not like the medical ones. The training at some places was only a matter of months before you were actually handling patients.

"Under supervision, of course," the actress said. "This isn't L.A. Out there all you need is the money for the Yellow Pages ad: QUALIFIED PSYCHOTHERAPIST, MARITAL, SEXUAL AND PERSONALITY PROBLEMS SOLVED SWIFTLY . . . VISA, MASTERCARD AND AMERICAN EXPRESS.'

She could joke because she didn't quite take Katherine's desperation seriously. No one did. Perhaps that's why Katherine had to escalate. What do you do after you've had crying jags on a P.E.N. Club panel at Carnegie Hall; when you've called the same friends at 4:00 A.M. threatening self-destruction one too many times?

What you do is you forget that you have left your baby in the affectionate care of the hat check people during lunch at the Russian Rendezvous, go on your way to a gallery opening, then run back to the restaurant sweating terror.

The first parapraxis was checking the book in its Scribner's shopping bag and forgetting to pick it up. Freud's book was to be her new primer. Myrna naturally knew nothing of all this when she handed it back to Katherine the next time she was in the restaurant. The writer stared at the book, distracted. But it was nothing to attract Myrna's attention.

People forget everything in check rooms, often the things most precious to them. Pianists forget sheet music, dancers forget leg warmers and love letters, singers forget the portfolios of reviews with which they were to dazzle impresarios.

People also forget gloves, coats, hats, packages of condoms, eyeglasses, wallets both empty and stuffed with money, appointment books with irreplaceable addresses and unlisted phone numbers, the lack of which can harm a career.

It was doubtful, however, if anyone had ever checked a child before. Later, when it all became an open secret, the Russian Rendezvous Regulars debated the point. The actress and teacher Stella Adler, grand and witty as usual, said the world would be a better place if more mothers had forgotten more children in coat rooms. Her husband, Harold Clurman, claimed to know an actress who had left her baby at Sardi's, in the days when people still went to Sardi's, but it was not a forgetting, it was an abandonment. The young woman had been driven insane by bad reviews of her first starring role and blamed the distractions of motherhood for the disaster.

Some of the regulars from the G.O.P., the Grand Old Period, believed that Myrna had as much to do with the developing events as the distracted mother and the adaptable child. That school of thought held that Myrna, disappointed in the way her life was going, jumped at the chance to raise Tulip in loco parentis. It was a chance to combine all her frustrated yearnings into one: she'd been a schoolteacher in Fargo, North Dakota, had come East to attack the stage, and become engaged to Sheffield, a director who had never directed a play but who made much of the fact that his sperm count was too low for fathering. (Just in case Myrna might press that issue.)

Mysteriously, Myrna became pregnant and had to take the job at the Russian Rendezvous to pay for the abortion he insisted she have. (During the Grand Old Period abortions were still illegal, dangerous, and expensive.) After she'd thrown him out he often came back to borrow money and to lecture her. Myrna was a soft touch.

"You're crazy, arranging study, play, and education of a four-year-old in a restaurant, with or without the mother's cooperation. You'll destroy the child and get yourself in hot water. You're trying to be a teacher, actress and earth mother all in one." (He'd never gotten to direct a play so he had to use psychology somewhere.)

But by that time the comedy had begun.

None of this could have happened without the ironic but careful complicity of K.K. Krasner, actor, and cashier at the Russian Rendezvous.

Krasner had a simple, fastidious contempt for the ballet of winning and losing that was performed, daily, in that dining room. His ambition was Shakespearian in its size and intensity; he could afford an Olympian gaze at people who tried to beat their friends out for a television commercial assignment with the passion of Richard the Third. You can see the re-runs of Krasner playing Coriolanus and other such sentimental softies on public television at least once every season. But as a famous actor he's no loftier, no more aristocratic, than he was when elegantly sliding the checks under the register and punching the keys. (Charge cards were less ubiquituous in those days—and Lew allowed personal charge accounts for the old customers, long after it was clear they would never be settled or even substantially reduced.)

Krasner was so cool you could never have guessed that he was worried. But he was. He was one of the few who knew what trouble the restaurant was getting into.

Lew and his co-owner, Paul Buchalter, were doing the classic partner act: fights, threats, reconciliations, and more fights. Buchalter was a vanilla business man—married, conservative. Lew was unhappy, lonely, drinking too much, and refusing to think of his restaurant as a business.

"This is not a Temple of the Arts and it's not a halfway-house for refugees," Buchalter began, right in front of the cashier's cage. It happened to be the first day of Katherine forgetting Tulip, but that was not yet an issue. Krasner watched from behind his silver-rimmed glasses and behind his cage, like a detached deity.

"Don't tell me what my place is," Lew said. "You bought in, you can buy out. This isn't your life, it's your investment."

All this, you understand, during the last few minutes of the rush lunch hour. (Though the RR was not yet the great success it is today. This scene couldn't happen quite that way now; there would be a line of people waiting to get a table.)

"You don't have the right spirit to run a good restaurant."

"You mean I don't have the soul of a headwaiter."

At which Misha, one of the twin headwaiters—the shy one—left for urgent mythical business in the kitchen, an action he performed whenever any difficulty arose in the front.

Ah, Lew Krale, restaurateur/laureate of our youth in New York; under your bleary eyes passed hundreds of the hopeful—deadbeat actors and writers supported by your willfull myopia regarding monthly bills. ("There are no deadbeats, only slowbeats," Lew said. "It might be ten years, but sooner or later everybody pays.") Restaurant Management for Poets, Paul called it.

Tulip, who had been following the argument with

interest, spoke up. "Which one," she asked Myrna, "is the headwaiter?"

"Oh, my God," Lew said. "What is that child doing here. This place used to have a liquor license."

He reached over the counter into the coat room and hauled Tulip up in his arms, surprising everyone.

"Who's mother are you?" he said to Tulip.

"Katherine Eudemie," she said.

"See that," Lew said. "The kid took my joke, treated me like I was dyslectic, reversed my reversal back, and told me who her mother is."

One of the best kept secrets in New York is that Lew Krale was a schoolteacher before he bought out the original owners of the RR. He'd actually published a paper on dyslexia.

It was that teacher of learning-disabled students— now they call it Special Ed—whose restaurant became the late-night hangout for two decades of playwrights (hit and flop)—produced, unproduced, and never to be produced. Also, the famous of all disciplines: Balanchine, Agnes de Mille; Arthur Miller, Harold Clurman, Eli Wallach, Anne Jackson, Dustin Hoffman, Lenny Bernstein—the semi-famous: Merce Cunningham, Kermit Bloomgarden—the obscure—how compile a list of the authentically obscure? Meade Roberts, the minor playwright, Larry Rosenthal, the minor composer, Sherwood Arthur, the minor director. (It is not enough to be not well known to merit the term obscure—one must have the possibility, the gifts that could have brought fame but by luck, character, or the nature of individual talent never did.)

The names don't sing the song; not even the ones you might recognize. (Those change from decade to decade, anyway. Who remembers Louis Spohr? In certain years of the nineteenth century he was as famous as Beethoven.) No! Much more important is the melody of the discourse at 12:45 A.M., fifteen minutes before closing time. Not a salon, exactly—not the Dome or La Coupole in 1945 with Sartre or Camus, but if less than that, more than Sardi's, more than sexual gossip and the ups and downs of careers. Laughter, literary and theatrical criticism, bad taste, cripple-jokes, philosophical questioning, career-pushing, psychoanalytical reflections, and the persistent borrowing of cash. "Ah," Stella Adler said, breathless one night, "we'll laugh our lives away." All of it washed with the light colors of youth and hope.

And all presided over, in a half-haze of alcohol, by Lew, the former teacher of the learning-disabled. And who could be more weirdly disabled than these wonderfully gifted loonybirds—winners and losers alike—staying up night after night making the least of their gifts . . . talking non-stop . . . laughing . . .

Jackson Eudemie had been one of them, happily peripheral. Neither obscure nor famous, he was just a young man mad about writing. He'd brought his young wife, Katherine, a refugee from the Wasp Middle West, into the RR circle. Somehow it closed with her inside and Jackson out. That's how it is with circles, the geometry of luck.

Lew made his restaurant a home away from home for these walking wounded. And he knew Katherine Eudemie to be the prime sort of gifted nut who helped give the restaurant its special texture. But children— this was another matter.

"Poor kid," he murmured over Tulip's blonde head. He handed her back to Myrna.

"Myrna," he said. "We don't check kids. Only hats and coats."

Buchalter didn't need much to push him over the line. He was a very short man, nervous to a fault. "Okay," he said. "That does it for me. Count me out."

Lew laughed. "One," he said, "two . . . three . . ." By this time his partner was gone through the revolving door.

Tulip was no dope. She showed how well she could count. "Four," she said, "five . . . six . . ."

Krasner didn't like Lew's laugh. He needed his cashier's job to pay bills while he searched out his dramatic destiny. "Are you sure you know what you're doing?" he asked. He pointed in the direction Buchalter had gone, the great outside world. "He won't just let it go. He'll counterattack! You don't want to lose your restaurant, do you?"

His bony face had turned pink at the emotional strain of making such a speech. Everyone knew that the cashier/actor could not make a speech longer than a half dozen words, usually short, caustic words; except when acting. What he required was a Shakespearian quotation, behind which he could hide true sentiments otherwise unavailable to his own natural tongue. He was known to be absolutely unwilling to read "cold" auditions. He left his nine-by-twelve glossies and resumes at production offices but never stayed to confront a living producer or casting director—anyone who might engage him in speeches of terrifying unpredictable length and potential sincerity. Whether this was the loftiness of a Coriolanus or Woody Allen shyness none of us knew. It was certainly one of the main reasons behind Krasner's lagging acting career.

"Misha," Lew called out, embarrassed at such passion from the cashier's cage, "Get a plate of sour cream for the kid and a Scotch for me."

"I'll get the sour cream for the girl but you've had enough to drink."

"Ah, then you're not Misha. You're Morris."

One of Lew's afflictions was having inherited twin headwaiters—identical twins, Misha and Morris. Bright, young refugees, no one knew exactly from where, Morris was a kind of self-appointed policeman of Lew's soul and was taking some course of study, as was his brother. No one knew what course, only that they spelled each other on nights—or days—when the other one was at school. Misha had no interest in Lew's drinking habits or his soul. That was Morris's territory. And Lew's torture was that he never knew which one he was yelling at.

"That happens to be true," Morris said. "But it doesn't change the facts: you've had enough."

"A Scotch, I said, Morris the miser, it's my Scotch and my life," Lew thundered. Morris brought the smallest Scotch he could pour.

Which Lew sipped while watching an hysterical Katherine return to clutch her daughter to her breast, her cheek, her lips.

"Tulip . . . Tulip . . ." she murmured, weeping in a combination of relief and embarrassment, "My God, my God, I'm so glad you're here."

"What does it all mean?" Lew muttered.

The next time the child was forgotten she was left for most of the afternoon. By the time Katherine Eudemie came back and got her, Tulip was helping Myrna with the early evening cocktail arrivals; no coats, the weather was warm, but there was a man's hat, there was a woman's attaché case. Sasha had begun to tell Tulip about the Chauve Souris, about what it was like to flee the Russian revolution, to join a song and dance troupe in Paris and end up in America in 1924. "You know what was the Chauve Souris?" Sasha asked. Tulip did not know. "My, my, my," Sasha said. Every little girl in White Russian circles in Paris had known of the Chauve Souris. When Katherine Eudemie arrived, the little girl was reluctant to leave. She asked her mother if she had ever heard of the Chauve Souris.

Katherine gave both women a sharp look but this time was not hysterical. For a brief moment it was not certain how the incident was to be treated.

"Please," Katherine said to Sasha, "don't fill her head with fairy tales"; a Russian noblewoman speaking to one of the women-in-waiting at her country estate. Then she and Tulip were gone and the evening business occupied everyone's attention.

It was Lew's lightness with Katherine's unpaid bills which fueled the first stages of the madness. She would never have thought to make a special trip to drop the child off at the coat room for the afternoon. But, lunching there almost every day as she did on her unpaid charge account, it grew easier and easier to just move on to her appointments and come back later and later. Precisely the kind of lunching Buchalter decided had to stop if they were to get the restaurant safely in the black.

This was New York of long ago, a city waking up from the dream of war. But the boom was losing some of its thunder. By the time of Katherine Eudemie's first parapraxis words like recession were in the air. Everyone knew somebody who knew somebody who had folded a business: a publishing house, a small record company, something! One heard distant rumors about established restaurants growing shaky, God forbid!

"Why does she do it?" Sasha asked Myrna.

"It doesn't matter. I wish she'd do it again."

"Don't wish such a thing."

"I can take care of her better."

"This is not right," Sasha said and turned to her Russian language newspaper.

"Everything isn't right," Myrna said. "For me to be alone in the world isn't right either. But I am. For Lew to be without a wife and to maybe lose his restaurant isn't right either, but it might happen."

"Bite your tongue," Sasha said.

Myrna smiled and waited for the next parapraxis.

How many times had Krasner heard Lew Krale muttering his favorite litany: *What does it all mean?* Once he pointed out to Lew that he had never once heard any of the questing artists who were drinking their drinks or stuffing their faces at the RR cry out What does it all mean? Only Lew, the owner, the businessman.

"Does that make you an artist manqué, Lew?" he asked.

"If I'm anything, I'm a businessman manqué." Lew laughed and said, "Get out of here and stop trying to make a manqué out of me."

Lew was devoted to failure. At first he did not know this, but later he got the idea quite clearly, and it became a kind of cause celebre for him. In spite of the superstars surrounding him, Lew would have liked to be the Saint of Failure. But that was to be denied him, like so many other things he wanted.

Lew: "What I love about these maniacal writers, these dancers especially, these musicians, is that they fail!

It's practically guaranteed. But they don't stop! They're crazy. They just don't give up. Krasner—(he was talking to the cashier at the end of the day)—some of them know they're doing their absolute best and they still fail! WHAT FUCKING HEROES!"

Krasner: "So?"

Lew: "If they lose and keep on going, why shouldn't I? Okay, a restaurant is not a play or a painting or a book. But it's a THING! IT'S A WAY OF BEING IN THE WORLD! And I want to go on like them, win or lose."

Krasner: "No dice, Lew. It doesn't work. Meat spoils. Sour cream goes bad. Lunches are down from last year and the cost of veal is up. It's not the same."

Lew (Mutters): "What does it all mean? Where are we all going?"

It's not clear what Katherine Eudemie's continuing parapraxes had to do with it, but came the first of July, when Myrna and Sasha would normally have been shifted from the coat check room and put to work elsewhere in the restaurant, they were told to stay put. You don't need coat check service, you need air conditioning. But Tulip's mother was maybe on the fourth or fifth parapraxis by then. No one in the restaurant was surprised at Lew's decision to keep Myrna and Sasha on duty in the front. It was a statement about the child's continuing presence and the new comedy of mistakes and affections.

Myrna was not insensitive to the subtle gift from Lew. It came with responsibilities.

"What's this prayer book doing here?"

"To teach the child about God."

"Sasha, she's only four years old."

"For four years old is no God?"

"No," Myrna said firmly. "God starts at seven. Tops. Maybe eight. And He will be brought in by her parents, if and when."

"Seven!" Sasha looked doubtful.

"It's not a question of does He exist or not. You were an actress, Sasha. Just make believe he's waiting in the wings."

"How long He waits?"

"Our father," Tulip chimed in.

Myrna grabbed her in a hug.

"Okay, wise guy, if you're so smart, who's Our Father?"

Tulip thought. "My father is Jackson Eudemie," she said. "So I guess Our Father is somebody else. But why is He waiting with wings?"

"You see?" Myrna said helplessly.

Sasha folded her Russian newspaper and added it to a floppy pile of papers on the shelf where, as the year progressed, hats would ultimately be kept. She took the prayer book and placed it on top of the day's paper. Then she went back to the kitchen to get three glasses of tea. She paraded in quiet, round triumph. Leaving Myrna with a new sense of the problems which might be coming at her from every unexpected direction. Her heart was beating hard as if she'd had a narrow escape.

TAKING TULIP TO THE BATHROOM. This proved to be not as traumatic as everyone had feared. Misha, who was on, stood guard while Myrna taught Tulip the basic ropes of restaurant ablutions. The child needed some help, but only the bare mechanics. Of course these were ordinary healthy times. Diarrhea waited, like God, in the wings.

*   *   *

Then there were Krasner's unspoken but intense concerns about the police. Captain Kolevitch dropped in often, a slender, nervous man with an enormous Saroyan-mustache, abandoned playwriting ambitions behind him, and a wife in and out of institutions. Lew knew him well. You couldn't run a restaurant without knowing the police.

"It's like running a whorehouse," Lew said. "It goes with the territory."

"Watch your mouth," Myrna said.

Lew looked at her with fresh interest.

"The kid is not here," he said. "Her mother took her back two hours ago. You're really getting into this, aren't you?"

"Listen," Myrna said. "She'll be back. I don't want you to get into bad habits. We're running a different kind of show now."

"Aha," Lew said.

"The problem is not Lew's mouth," Krasner said. "It's Captain Kolevitch."

"I can't take a man seriously whose name sounds like a dish on my menu," Lew said.

"Mistake," Krasner said. "What's in a name?"

"We are not discussing roses, we're talking Tulip."

"Just everybody keep their mouth shut that we have a kid in the coat room okay?" This sentence, at least nine words longer than Krasner's usual, made everybody take the Tulip/security question seriously. Captain Kolevitch was greeted with an odd ceremoniousness on his next visit. It made him suspicious and he resolved to check out what was happening at the Russian Rendezvous more closely.

Lew Krale felt more at home in his restaurant than in his home. With a customer he liked—a rare bird, but

occasionally to be found—after the coffee, dessert, and
check he would stand up and see him to the door as
if he were in his own home. But on the odd chance
you were invited to his apartment down on West Tenth
Street in the Village, he might fall asleep if the drinking
and the laughing had been heavy, and leave you to
find your way out unescorted. Home is where the heart
beats and the RR raced Lew's pulse.

A Tulip-Moment: Agnes de Mille heading for the exit,
enraged at having been seated in the back near the
men's room, looking for sympathy, looking for Lew or
Misha, comes upon Tulip at exactly the same moment
Georges Balanchine enters the RR.

"Hello, young woman," Balanchine said, bending over
the ledge of the coat room to observe Tulip more closely,
(it came out vooman), "Do you dance?"

Agnes de Mille, still flushed and angry snapped at
him, "Georges, she's too young for the bar."

"Merde," Balanchine said, staring past her at old
dance world resentments, Bolshoi versus Broadway to
get it down to simplicities. "I started Natasha Makharova
at three."

"And where is she now?"

"She stopped dancing."

"Aha!"

"Aha, nothing. She got married."

"Why not," Agnes de Mille said. "You do it all the
time."

"I do it to dancers."

"Exactly so," Agnes de Mille said and turning to
Myrna she said, "Your little girl must start dancing
now. Four years old is already late."

Tulip, in high spirits at all this attention, turned and

turned in a graceful pastiche of ballet. The Eudemies
had a television set; Tulip had observed.

"No," Agnes de Mille said, "Not now, just soon. I'll
teach you first position next time I come."

Balanchine was gone. His swift disappearance was
disapproval. Agnes de Mille went on to seek Misha, in
Lew's absence, to complain of once again being seated
near the Men's Room, but, today, Misha turned out to
be Morris. Baffled, she swept out. Perhaps only a dancer
can sweep out through a revolving door.

Myrna, proud of Tulip in advance, experienced a
tremble, a little frisson of what mothers must feel.
("Your little girl must start dancing now . . .) It made
her breath rush in a thrill through her breast.

Not long after her excitement at being mistaken for
Tulip's mother she was called upon to explain the
grown-up world, a little, to the kid. Which is, of course,
one of the main things mothers do, either by example
or using words.

It was harder than Myrna had imagined. A tart little
dose of reality.

One early evening a woman was turned away from
the bar because she was unescorted. The woman did
not look especially disreputable. Somebody from a very
small midwestern town might have felt the lipstick did
not outline the lips closely enough, that the hair was
too frizzy, and the perfume too heavy. But basically
she was middle-class: a secretary, a saleswoman, a
housewife out for an evening: ambiguous. Still, off the
premises she must go and without any real explanation.
But not without a fuss.

When it was over Tulip wanted an explanation.

Myrna fumbled, stammered, and said, "Sometimes

bad women come to sit alone and talk to men they
don't know, instead of coming here with men they know
or they're married to . . . And then a restaurant gets
to be a bad hangout and the regular customers stop
coming . . ."

Tulip's steady gaze, her waiting for Myrna to make
some sense out of nonsense, froze Myrna's tongue. Suddenly she realized how dumb all this was and how easy
it is to lie to children.

"Listen," she said. "It's because men aren't fair to
women."

"I'm a woman," Tulip said.

"Well—yes," Myrna said.

"Will I be able to sit a bar without a man when I
grow up?"

"Unless they keep having one law for the lion and
one for the lamb."

"Am I a lion?"

"Certainly not!"

"Am I a lamb?"

"Just hang up this coat and shut your lamb chop."

Myrna was embarrassed. In that internal theater in
which we all perform our play with ourselves as audience, she'd caught herself dumbly accepting something she'd always known was bullshit. You could usually tell a professional and it was no trick to keep the
place from becoming a hooker hangout.

It was just men fucking women over as usual.

Playing "mother" was instructive.

"Don't be afraid, kid. I'm drunk but I'm a different
kind of drunk."

"Lew . . ." Myrna said.

"I'm Jewish. A special breed. Alcoholicus Judaicus.

Gentle, self-punishing only, guilty but not angry. And, most important of all, sooner or later I get hungry."

Tulip was curious. "All people get hungry."

"Not drunks. But *I* always stop drinking and start eating."

"Are you hungry now?"

"It's not going to be that easy, tonight," Lew said. "Not tonight."

Myrna observed and drew conclusions. From being apprehensive and even angry about Tulip's presence in the restaurant, Lew had grown to like having her around. An odd painting was being sketched in Myrna's soul: an ersatz Renaissance picture, The Negative Holy Family. A man who wasn't her husband, a child who wasn't her child, and Myrna/Madonna.

The summer sun was warming up the New York streets. Fantasies of strolls in the park chased around in Myrna's thoughts. She thought of mentioning some of this to Krasner but was embarassed at the thought of exposing herself. Suppose people thought she was using Tulip to get closer to Lew? A sense of shame expressed itself swiftly in a decision to make phone calls to agents. The summer stock season was all booked, but the fall productions would be getting under way soon. Her ex-lover, Sheffield, was as much a fantasy as all of this. She had to get on with Real Life.

Besides, the RR lunch business was off so badly, who knew if she would still have a job in the fall? The telephone was in the rear of the restaurant. But en route she fell into a conversation with Gregor, a roly-poly veteran waiter. They discussed rumors: Paul was about to make an offer to buy Lew's share, take over again, get rid of the nonpaying regulars and change everything. By the time she remembered the original purpose of her errand she saw a familiar shaggy gray head—premature but startlingly gray—up front. It was

Sheffield, her ex-lover who refused to accept his termination; and who stopped by to deliver lectures to Myrna, borrow money from her, or both. Myrna not only had no money to lend him, she realized she'd forgotten to bring change for the phone.

So, for the moment, that was that on the Real Life front.

We have to imagine Katherine Eudemie waking in the middle of the night in a sweat of terror. We have to imagine her lying for a moment next to Jackson Eudemie sleeping his usual tranquil sleep, hers so palpable, a kind of semi-suffocation of snores, dreams that force gasps and waking instead of protecting sleep, and imagine her grabbed by panic before she realizes what the panic is about.

Then she gropes for her long white robe, almost tripping on the belt, and runs into Tulip's bedroom. The little girl sleeps the innocent sleep of one who can tell Misha from Morris, infallibly. It astonishes everyone, this gift of hers; no one can explain it. The mysteries of identical twinness do not exist for Tulip. Some of the more imaginative members of the RR inner circle think of this as a kind of grace. Lew thinks it is only a series of lucky guesses. But he is impressed.

Of course Katherine does not know any of this. She only knows that her life is racing out of control; that she runs her daily rat race, writing her new novel, chasing assignments at *The New York Times Book Review* so that she won't be forgotten between books, terrified that she has already been forgotten after the fuss that greeted her first book four years ago, showing up for her analytic training classes—she has not missed one, though she now doubts the auspices and wonders if it is all legitimate, perhaps only another mad dance to distract herself from her own frantic dance, never missing her exercise class, because the body might be all that is left if the mind and the talent go; scared, too, that forgetting her child at the restaurant is no longer a mistake—something much worse. She has begun to masturbate in the bathrooms of midtown restaurants and art galleries.

We must imagine that she picks the sleeping Tulip up and holds her, crooning, wetting the shut eyes with tears, unable to imagine a time when Tulip had not been with her as pride and comfort.

The next afternoon she forgets her at the RR for the longest stretch ever: five hours.

Studying the text she'd once forgotten at the restaurant, *The Psychopathology of Everyday Life* by Sigmund Freud, reading about the forgetting of proper names—and how complicated the causes of such simple lapses could be— Katherine Eudemie marvels and despairs at the language of gestures and at what the language of the repeated forgetting of a child might mean. Reading the book and thinking about her own lapses she feels a shiver of terror.

Katherine Eudemie's therapist was a woman who smoked cigarette after cigarette, a bad sign Katherine thought. "Listen," she said, "I'm not sure this is going to work out."

"Oh?"

"Remember the time I told you about, when I left my child at the hat check room of the Russian Rendezvous?"

"I remember that time, yes."

"Those times!"

"Oh . . ."

"Yes."

"You left her or 'forgot' her?"

"The first time, definitely forgot. The second time, pretty surely. The last few it became a kind of collaboration. The women in the hat check room seem to like taking care of Tulip. But it scares me. That's why I'm not sure this is going to work out."

"What is 'this'?"

"The treatment, the training. I'm a patient, not vice-versa."

"You know, you shouldn't confuse what we're doing here with a classical, full-fledged Training Analysis. There is a certain way of life in America's Big Cities, New York, Chicago, L.A. (the therapist had a way of speaking in capital letters which unnerved Katherine), in which people like you and I—writers whose careers disappoint, actresses whose parts never quite get recognized, the wives of successful painters who feel overlooked, mothers who have survived mortal combat with their daughters who are now off in College—all of us having had lots of treatment of different kinds, decide to become therapists. It's as much a statement about the impossibility of being a Middle-Class Woman in Modern America as it is a fresh career start." Pause to light a new cigarette from the embers of the old. Katherine sits, stunned. "I'm telling you all this to lower your expectations. You're not going to be a Healthy Individual Curing Patients."

"Then—what?"

"You're going to understand a little more about yourself and spend your time more fruitfully than hanging around waiting for your next novel to be rejected. You'll help some patients and not others and you'll earn money, maybe even a living. Best of all, you'll be doing actively to others what you experienced passively for so many years."

"What's that?"

"TREATMENT!"

"Even if I'm so crazy myself?"

"You said the others at the restaurant were collaborating with you in this."

"Yes . . ."

"So who's crazy, you or them or everybody? We're talking about the text you're studying: *The Psychopathology of Everyday Life*. Everybody is disappointed in something from infancy on—everybody has a vested interest in forgetting, distorting, or ignoring reality so that it feels better for the moment. This gets worse as the years mount up."

"Is that what's going on here?"

"That's what's going on here."

"Ah . . ."

She stubbed a cigarette out in a flash of red and said, in her Feminist Voice: "It's a General Breakdown, but as always Women lead the way."

"Ah . . ." Katherine said again. She felt better.

Myrna, too, felt better, central after years of feeling peripheral. She was the only one feeling better. As the summer burned toward mid-August, the desired pre-fall upturn in business did not happen. Krasner tallied lunch totals and Lew pondered a new advertising campaign, but he was too paralyzed by his troubles to take effective action. Paul's lawyers made rumbling noises in the background.

*   *   *

It's hard to pinpoint exactly when the story of Tulip, Katherine Eudemie, and the Russian Rendezvous began to make its way into the air. There's always such a moment; it may be created by random gossip, by observation, or by someone purposely spreading the story for reasons of their own. It is already making the rounds when Jackson Eudemie enters his old hangout, the Russian Rendezvous, and the central action of the story, carrying a suitcase and looking for Lew Krale.

"It's been a long time, Jackson," Lew said. "Put your suitcase in the check room."

"No thanks, I'll hold onto it. How are you Lew?"

"No way you'd know," Lew said with typical tact. "What'll you have?"

"It's a little early in the day," Jackson Eudemie said. "I'll have some tea."

"Misha," Lew said. "One tea and one Scotch."

"Two teas coming up!"

"Dammit, Morris! If that's you—a tea and a Scotch or I'll eat your bones for dinner."

Then, to Jackson, with ominous weight, "So, stranger . . ."

"Listen, Lew," Jackson Eudemie said, "My life's different, now."

"You mean money?"

"Right."

"Wrong. You know I never gave a damn about your bills. Think about all those nights we closed this place, together. You wrote a whole novel here on the arm."

"It's different when you're married."

"Hold it," Lew said. "Harold was married, Zero was married . . ."

"There's married and there's married," Jackson Eudemie said. "They were married. I got married."

"I know," Lew said, defeated. "But don't use the money as an excuse for vanishing from the scene."

"It's mainly that Katherine is in trouble—and there's my kid . . ."

"I know," Lew said to his glass.

"You're a bachelor, Lew, you'll understand. I never thought I'd get married. The thing was to be a great writer. But it all got reversed. I'm a married man who's a small-fry litterateur."

"What the hell is that?"

"A literary man of small caliber. My father used to own guns. They scared the hell out of me. But so did my father. Well, if I were a pistol, I'd be a .22; not even a .38 and certainly not a .45; just a .22."

Lew was thoughtful. "I don't think there's any such weapon as a .22 pistol. I think that's a kid's air rifle—but I wouldn't swear to it.

"Aha!" Jackson said. "You see my point. Here I am—a nonexistent .22 caliber anthologist, trying to be a responsible family man with a wife who was—albeit briefly—a .45 pistol, dynamite on the scene . . . Then the dynamite turns wet . . . she has a baby . . . then after a time turns desperate . . . even a little strange . . . I'll tell you, Lew, there's more going on . . ."

"Oh?"

"She's not up to the mark."

"I got the idea," Lew said.

"No . . . she's not well. We don't know everything yet—but something serious may be happening."

"Shit," Lew said.

"I'm worried."

Not knowing what else to say, Lew said, "How is it with you two?"

"Off . . . way off . . . It has been for years." Long

before this medical stuff started. I got married for the wrong reasons."

"That's a membership in a very large club."

"She was so pretty and so ready to eat up New York. Then she got eaten up . . . Maybe I will have a drink . . ."

"Have a Moscow Mule for old time's sake. Morris," Lew called out, then said, "Never marry a disappointed person."

"People aren't born disappointed. Things don't pan out. Then comes regret and it poisons everything."

Lew nodded and kept his peace.

"I used to have low expectations of life," Jackson said.

"A wonderful way to be."

"I didn't know what to expect of marriage. But it started to go bad long before this new stuff—leaving Tulip, trying to become a therapist."

"A what? I thought she was always on the couch herself?"

"Don't be so surprised. Patients and therapists are like the cops and the Mafia. Two sides of the same coin."

"Too glib, Jackson," Lew said. "Norman Mailer baloney."

"Katherine has a thing for Mailer. She says he's a part Jew, the same as her."

"As she," Lew said.

"Okay, Professor."

"And Mailer is all Jewish. All Brooklyn."

"I know what she means. He's Jewish but doesn't really care to be."

"And your wife?"

"You don't know what it's like to live with a midwestern Wasp woman who thinks the sun rises and sets on New York Jewish intellectuals and writers."

"A pretty good group, all in all," Lew said.

"FANTASTIC!" Jackson cried out. "Who's going to argue with Delmore Schwartz or Bernard Malamud or Lionel Trilling . . . ? I can't argue BUT I CAN'T BE ONE OF THEM, EITHER!"

"Take it easy, Jackson . . ."

"I do, I do, that's the trouble. Real easy. My style is light and I am not filled with *angst* . . ."

"What is angst?" Lew asked. "I see it printed all the time and I never think to look it up."

"Don't worry—you've got plenty. It's just the German word for anxiety with a capital A. Which doesn't mean that *only* Jews have it." No culture without anxiety.

"We had culture," Jackson said. "My father, Insurance Man, Canadian Goy, but we were poor. Jews don't have a monopoly on poverty, you know."

"You were talking about culture." Lew was wary now.

"Before stereo, before hi-fi, we had a phonograph— a shabby street in Vancouver but we had chamber music records. My parents bought sets of Dickens and Mark Twain from the local newspaper with coupons, book by book. Sunday afternoons, Schubert's C Major Quintet blooming in the air, me as confused as any Jewish adolescent intellectual . . . masturbating as much as Phillip Roth . . ."

"This is some club you feel so left out of," Lew said.

"Only since Katherine. I came to New York. She came to New York. But it was different."

"All immigrants."

"But she came looking for her Jews."

"No shortage here. They thin us out a lot, most other places."

"It hurts, Lew, being married to a woman who has energy and talent and who thinks I'm some Canadian variety of white bread."

"Is it true? Are you?"

"No! There've been times when I thought I was going insane . . ."

"That's good. Check one."

"Times when I thought I'd written something pretty damned fine."

"Check two," Lew said. "But you may just have it all backwards. What you need to qualify are times when you thought you were the only sane person in the world."

Jackson shook his head, hopeless.

Lew went on. "Times when you thought you'd written the worst piece of *drek* ever put on paper?"

"No."

"Sorry, Jackson." Lew says, solemn. "You're just a little too comfortable in your skin."

"I've written twelve books. Okay, edited . . ."

"Forget it!"

"I had a poem in *The Hudson Review* when I was a senior at Yale."

"No dice."

"I don't drink—hardly at all."

"Give it up!"

"What's the matter, Lew. You think I'm too dumb?"

Lew clutches his forehead. "Are you kidding?" he says. "Do you know how many words there are in Yiddish for a dope?"

"No idea."

"A million. Did you ever hear of a *yutz*?"

"No."

"A *yold*?"

More astonishment. "No!"

"You see what a sheltered life you've had. A *schmuck*?"

"That one I know."

"Not fair. That's in the language by now. How about a *naar*?"

"A what?"

"Drop it, Jackson. If you knew them all, it wouldn't make any difference. Frankly, even if you were Jewish, you wouldn't be Jewish."

Jackson is dazed by how close to the bone this discussion of his fate has come. Katherine found, Katherine lost; the shadow-Jew he could not be . . . He murmurs, "You don't know how it hurts . . ."

"Pain I know," Lew says. "Everybody has pain. But you have to face it, my friend. YOU ARE AT EASE IN ZION."

Jackson stood up. In spite of his sober claims, the floor was unsteady.

"I'm sorry," Lew said. "I didn't mean to hurt your feelings."

Jackson groped for the suitcase he'd brought with him. "Listen, Lew, I'm worrying about more than hurt feelings. This is life and death. I'm not fighting what's been going on here. I can't. So, I guess I'm joining it." He threw an arm wave at the coat room.

"Joining or resigning?" Lew says.

"Listen, I've got a deadline for an anthology of Chassidic Love Poems for Dodd Mead."

At Lew's quizzical look he offers, "It's a dirty job but somebody's got to do it. It means library research hours, xeroxing, editing . . . I can't afford a housekeeper to take care of Tulip and I never even know where Katherine is any more."

He stands up and starts an odd retreat toward the revolving door. He pauses to finish his tea and puts it on an empty table. Myrna appears from behind her barrier and scoops it up—an excuse to be close to the action, nothing more.

"We love Tulip and she's been thriving here, so . . ."

He thrusts the suitcase in the general direction of his audience, which now includes Myrna, Lew, Krasner behind the cashier's cage, and Sasha, whose innocent outstretched arms finally receive the gift.

Lew finds a few words. "But how long—?"

"Well," Jackson said, he was at the door now. "After this I have to do a collection of Vietnam War Jokes for North Point Press . . ." The visit was over, leaving Myrna and Sasha to sort through the baby clothes and one pair of grown woman's panties stuck in by mistake.

Later that afternoon when Katherine Eudemie brought Tulip in, Myrna handed her the intimate item, tactfully placed in a Lord & Taylor shopping bag someone had left. Katherine Eudemie looked at it with a secret smile and said nothing.

Myrna was exultant.

The child!

Her clothes!

Permission from the father!

Everything was coming up Tulips!

One day in late September Myrna returned from the bathroom to find a small crowd clotting the area near the coat room.

Arbut Blatas, one of the Old Guard Regulars and the man who had painted the murals on the RR walls, had taught Tulip to say goodbye in Russian (das vedanya) and was in the process of teaching her the prologue to Pushkin's Ruslan and Ludmilla. Tulip spoke the sounds smashingly, "like a darlink Russian parrot," Blatas said admiringly.

A number of patrons lingered, unpaid checks in hand, to listen to the little girl repeat Russian poetry. Normally this would irritate Krasner; processing checks was his job. But this afternoon he was a Cheshire cat. His smile hovered blessing the little comedy in progress.

Myrna got the message. Only a few minutes before, she and Krasner had been kicking around the work situation, present and future, gloom and doom. Then, in a few swift taciturn Krasner-like images he had sketched out Operation Tulip. The word would be spread about the kid in the hat check room. People would tell each other. It would give curious New Yorkers and naive out-of-towners a rooting interest in coming—like a mascot on a football team. He didn't actually say all this because there was no appropriate quotation in blank verse for him to use, but Myrna got the idea.

"You're crazy," she said.

"Never mind," Krasner said. "I know a hawk from a halvah when the wind is North."

"I thought you were so worried about Captain Kolevitch finding out."

"One step at a time."

"You're crazy," Myrna said. "You can't use a kid to increase business."

Krasner didn't think much of this. "All grown-ups use kids for something. See Shaw—preface to *Misalliance*."

Myrna had turned away in confusion. Now she told Tulip, "You shouldn't say things you don't understand."

Scornfully, Tulip said, "*Das Vedanya* means "goodbye." In Russian. Mr. Blatas says a child can learn to speak a lot of languages."

Myrna shut up.

Krasner counted the house.

Then the real craziness began.

Katherine Eudemie came to the restaurant, without

Tulip, looking for Myrna, who was menstruating at the time and depressed. Always she had been sad at that time of the month. Later, when the two women were walking in Central Park, Myrna confided that she'd heard women were sad at that time of the month because they were mourning the loss of the birth possibility and Katherine said "Crap"—(like many of her women friends she liked to talk tough even though none of the men they liked talked that way.) "I never believed that stuff. That's only literature."

"I would have thought biology," Myrna said. "But I never took either." That was when Katherine Eudemie made the offer of payment. "No, no, don't look so horrified. It's not for helping to take care of Tulip. That would be like paying you for babysitting. You really care about Tulip. No, this is a genuine bribe."

"For what?"

"If Mr. Eudemie asks about Tulip spending a lot of time with you at the RR, just say—well, you can say the truth—that I've given you money for that. That it's not accidental or strange or anything."

Myrna laughed. They crushed dry leaves underfoot as they turned south back toward the park exit. It was chilly. Myrna's mind was a jumble. Depression was gone—so much for menstruation mythology. She decided not to tell Katherine Eudemie that her husband knew all about it, that he was now an accomplice, having added a suitcase full of Tulip's clothes to the conspiracy.

She said: "Here's what I'll do. If I take your money I won't say anything. But if I don't—and I won't—I'll be glad to tell your husband you are paying me to take care of Tulip. Okay?" Such are the deals made by everyday craziness. Katherine recognized the logic and instantly accepted it.

The two women strolled through the September light,

still a sort of straight sunshine, not yet the slanting light
of winter.

"What do you imagine is actually happening?" Kath-
erine Eudemie asked.
"Oh, I'm beyond imagining," Myrna said. "I'm just
grateful for Tulip."
"Do you see what I'm doing as something mad?"
"I see it as a—gift."
"In other words you're thinking about your own life;
not mine, not Tulip's mother . . ."
"I suppose I should be ashamed at my selfishness.
But I'm too desperate for that." Katherine looked at the
young woman. "You too," she said. "Is it possible that
every woman I meet these days is desperate?"
Myrna said she didn't know. She could only describe
her own situation . . . lost . . . the sense of time having
almost run out . . . herself grateful for a new, inspiriting
career, Tulip-raising.
"If anyone should be ashamed, it's me," Katherine
Eudemie said. "You're helping. I'm doing an imitation
of being helpless."
They were at the park playground. Puerto Rican
children climbed all over the statue of Alice In Won-
derland. The day became noisy.
"Is it an imitation? Myrna asked. "Or can you really
not help doing it?"
"I don't know," Katherine Eudemie said. "There's so
much masquerade in my life, anyway. All I know is
when I needed someone—and I didn't even know I
needed them—you were there. I've never been too good
at having friends. Emerson says the way to have a
friend is to be one. And I've had and lost so many."

She was speeding now, as she did a lot these days. "Do you have many friends?" she asked.

"No," Myrna said. "Not right now."

"Friends were such a comfort when I was a youngster."

"Me too," Myrna said. "Actors are always with friends—hanging out at coffee shops." She sighed a memory. "Whenever I smell coffee that's bitter from reheating I think of friends." Katherine Eudemie fixed Myrna with a stare that made Myrna nervous.

"I've been on the move so much," Katherine said, "My only friends have been my ambitions. I had an older man who guided me in Chicago—but we were lovers so—and then I came East. I HAVE TO DO SOMETHING WITH MYSELF BEFORE IT'S TOO LATE."

"I understand that," Myrna said, uneasy.

Katherine Eudemie grabbed her hand; on an impulse she held it to her lips.

"Can we be friends?" she said.

Myrna did not know where to look until she got her hand back. Then she said, "I don't really understand what's going on." And began to cry. Short quiet sobs. Katherine Eudemie held her until she stopped. Then they walked on talking and listening.

Myrna felt her life had all been a waiting game in which nothing added up to much until Tulip. There was no explaining why Tulip was the answer, since the question was so unclear. But there it was! Tulip was what had happened. It was as complicated and as simple as that. But that was the one thing you couldn't tell the child's own mother. Impossible to discuss the surprises of Tulip with her own forgetful lost mother, Tulip so found, her mother so lost. For a moment Myrna felt she loved Katherine Eudemie the way she loved Tulip. But it was only for a moment.

It had been spring when Katherine Eudemie's copy of *The Psychopathology of Everyday Life* had been forgotten; now it was fall.

Fall also brought an offer from Paul to buy out Lew's share of the RR.

"I'll keep paying that fat philistine forever before I'll give him a crack at this restaurant," Lew yelled into the phone. "Ask him if he'd like smaller bills so they'll fit better."

"Hey," the lawyer said. "Hey."

"Or maybe your client could lend me some money without interest just for auld lang syne?"

"Hey," the lawyer said. "Hey."

Myrna's obsession with Tulip grew with each passing parapraxis. But now it was split between kid and mother. Myrna read Katherine Eudemie's novel, *The Country of the Young.* She thought she'd never read such a beautiful book. Why, she wondered, wasn't it famous? Sometimes, when business was slow she read passages aloud to Tulip informing her that it was her mother's book.

"She did that before I was born," Tulip commented, placing the work in correct literary historical perspective.

Myrna also ran after dogs because Tulip ran after dogs. Lew didn't mind. He hated dogs in his restaurant. She also ran after 'cellos because Tulip did. (There were more such to worry about in the RR than there were dogs.) Both dog owners and 'cellists were charmed by Tulip and Myrna was made happy.

Krasner was livelier than usual, too. Operation Tulip was starting to work. The actor put together pages of numbers, hand-crampingly compiled—(B.C., Before Computers.)

"Lunches are up," he called out.

But when the afternoon light began to slant, when Tulip arrived wearing purple mittens and a matching wool scarf, bad news about Katherine Eudemie began to seep into the RR.

Someone mentioned sickness, someone else spoke of a diagnosis; someone even more else mentioned another diagnosis. Lew understood Jackson Eudemie's ambiguous but grim remarks the day he'd brought Tulip's clothes in. From the way things had run, Myrna expected something psychiatric. After all—forgetting a child, even once! . . . But fifty-six times!

What was needed was a confirmed diagnosis!

One such came from Joe Larrabie, Lew Krale's personal surgeon. Yes, Lew had such an animal. Not for himself, but for the regulars who needed medico-surgical advice. Not for Lew was the usual, "Ask your doctor." The RR was a complete life-support system, not just a restaurant. Hence Doctor Joe Larrabie with his own practice and his own table just at the entrance to the dining room.

It was Larrabie who passed along the awful diagnosis of cancer. He glanced around as he hissed the terrifying middle sibilant. By chance, neither Myrna nor Tulip was on the premises.

Only Lew and sly old Sasha heard Joe. The old Russian woman swallowed the fearful word with the stolid acceptance of age. *"Boije moy,"* she muttered; a familiar Russian incantation of woe to come and woe remembered.

Fatalism, okay! But what Imp of the Perverse made Sasha tell Myrna when she came on the next afternoon?

Sasha tells Myrna.

Myrna, despairing, tells Krasner.

Krasner's first thought is Jackson Eudemie. He assumes Jackson brought the suitcase full of Tulip's things knowing she needed a new home, soon to be motherless. "I know Jackson Eudemie," Krasner says, jowled with suspicion, "from the old days. Once a hanger-on, always."

Lew butts in. "You think Jackson's laying off his kid on us? Crazy!"

Krasner nods, rabbinic. "Everybody should be so crazy. Books and poetry but he lives." In Krasner shorthand this translated as: anybody who can actually make some kind of living by putting together anthologies of Chassidic Love Poems isn't so loony.

Myrna's heart slowed down in terror. Maybe Krasner was right. Not only the girl's father but even her mother must have known all along that they had an imminent orphan on their hands. Myrna remembered the fall afternoon Katherine Eudemie had sought her out offering her money and confiding her life story and her terrifying lapses of memory.

Parapraxis my ass! Myrna murmured. (Perhaps the first time in history the first and third word had ever been used in a single sentence.)

Katherine Eudemie's impending mortality changed everything. An impromptu Educational Planning Commission was set up. Music, art, dance, these were easy to come by at the RR. But what of science, what of English, what of math? Lessons were needed. But, for example, which—the New Math or the Old? There were so many issues to be decided. Being a parent was no easier when there were a dozen parents instead of the usual two.

Then, shortly after the terrible gossip circulated as fact, Myrna became a prisoner of her new obsession. Her insides moved in calligraphic certainty. The message was as clear as if the entrails of a chicken were spread out before a medieval rabbi: a childless destiny. There was no evidence; no cysts, no spotting; only an obsessive sense of permanent internal decay. The abortion sponsored by Sheffield and endured by her was much on her mind. Such an event was a permanent judgment, she decided. It had sealed her fate. She was so convinced she told no one.

The result was: Tulip became Myrna's last chance. The kidnapping which later astonished everyone was now inevitable. Thus are born future *New York Post* headlines:

ACTRESS SNATCHES KID FROM
POSH RESTAURANT

NOVELIST MOM MAKES POIGNANT PLEA
FROM HOSPITAL BED

The first heavy snow brought to New York the Asian flu Type B and Russian refugees of all types. One of them was Yuri Yevshenkowitz, a skinny chain-smoker from Moscow University, formerly a professor on the verge of a breakthrough paper in topology and now a waiter at the RR.

"Chulip," Yevshenkowitz said, "a/ex times the

square+=is how you arrive at the answer. I hed a
student in Moscow half your age. Well—"
"Tell me again," said Tulip who had not even de-
parted from the question. Myrna watched in despair.

"Eh, maintenant," the small bald man said to Tulip,
"Il faut que tu fasses ton leçon pour le jour. Répète,
Les sanglots longs des violons . . ."
"Les sanglots longs des violons . . ." Tulip murmured
in perfect imitation.
"Harold," he said, "Elle a une bonne oreille."
"Eugene," Clurman said, "Isn't she a little young for
Verlaine?"
"Jamais trop jeune pour Verlaine," Ionesco said. He
was in town for rehearsals of a new play and Clurman
thought it would be nice for Tulip to start learning
another language besides Russian. After rehearsals Io-
nesco would get slightly tipsy and start teaching. Once
Clurman caught him in an error of grammar. Ionesco
replied, "I am a Roumanian. We are not fanatics of
grammar as are the French." They were cheery sessions.
No one had told either of them about the condition of
Tulip's mother.
"The elongated sobs of the violins of autumn wound
my heart," Tulip recited happily in French. She bowed
and the entire bar area applauded. Myrna watched in
despair.

The day that Captain Kolevitch came for lunch, Tulip
was in the kitchen learning how to make chicken Kiev.
She didn't feel too well but she didn't want to spoil

her first cooking lesson. And she didn't want them to have to summon Myrna from the front.

"Congratulations," Lew said. It's Wednesday. The Siberian pelmeny is terrific today."

"Nu, Lew," Kolevitch said, "It's been a while."

"What's this 'nu'? You're not Jewish. I'm Jewish! You're of Ukranian anti-Semitic derivation."

"That's what made this country great. All of us living together. The place has changed."

"Yeah. We put Christmas decorations on the ceiling."

"I meant something much more profound. All these new faces."

"Which? What new?"

"Lew, I know this territory. Don't forget I wrote six unproduced plays before I decided to give it up and become a policeman. And two of them were as good as anything your snotnose off-broadway scribblers are doing today. So I know."

"Know what?"

"I know that the place is full of agents, suddenly. There's Sam Cohn, there's Flora what's-her-name? ICM, CAA, the restaurant is lousy with acronyms. Movies, plays. Also, Woody Allen has been seen here."

"Don't talk like a cop, Kolevitch. It's not a crime to be seen here."

"I was just making a point. It's different. It used to be hangers-on, schleppers. Emigré Russians, out-of-work actors."

"They're still here. I'm proud of their loyalty."

"Where are they?"

"Well—not at lunch so much. More late night."

A waiter appeared. "Can I get the Captain a drink before lunch?"

"I'm in uniform, schmuck. That means I'm on duty. Get me a water glass with vodka and some ice in it."

"Captain Kolevitch will have the pelmeny, Pierre,"

Lew said. "Make sure it's hot. And a double Scotch for me."

"You see." Kolevitch said.

"See what?"

"What kind of a Russian name is Pierre? Where's Gregory?"

"HE'S OFF TODAY. MY GOD. And Pierre was in *War and Peace!*"

"That reminds me," the policeman said. "Now there's the publishing crowd. Royalty conversations, paperback deals. Very chic, very in. No empty tables." He tossed back a quick swig of water/vodka.

"Come back on a Monday. What the hell are you nudging me about?"

"We had a tip about the kid in the restaurant, Lew. But that kitten has been out of that bag for some time."

"What kitten? What bag?"

Lew covered his confusion with Scotch. Kolevitch sipped his on-duty vodka like water.

"Lew," the policeman said, "Everybody knows about Operation Tulip."

"What operation?"

"How this kid is living in the restaurant—how you're taking care of her and she's taking care of you. You can't hide such a spectator sport. It's not good, Lew."

"It's not true, either!"

Kolevitch tossed off the rest of his vodka and signalled Pierre for more.

"We have a statement," he said. "Your hat check girl has a boyfriend. Had. He turned you in. The kid's name is—" pause to consult small notebook—"Tulip Eudemie."

"Aha!" Lew said, "Is that a real name? Tulip. A dumb story."

But he was defeated. He drank two glasses of Scotch before saying another word.

"This place," Kolevitch said, his mouth full of veal dumplings, "it means a lot to me."

"Yeah . . ."

"A shrine to my youthful hopes."

"You couldn't write," Lew said. "Somebody said you looked like Saroyan in your moustache so you wrote plays."

"Don't piss on my youth."

"Don't threaten my restaurant with anonymous informers."

"Not anonymous. Name is Sheffield." Another glass of vodka vanished.

In desperate distraction Lew said, "How's your poor Helen?"

Kolevitch shook his head, hopeless.

"I'm sorry to hear that."

"She'll never get straightened out. She sang her song and now she's lost the tune."

"Those Laughing Academies are awful," Lew said, hoping for a reprieve if not a full pardon. "They could kill the song in a nightingale."

"And you should know what they cost."

The two middle-aged men lean over the plates of soups and sour cream in the middle of the table, wrung by their separate griefs.

"I'm happy for the turnaround, Lew, and for you," Kolevitch says. "But it cannot go on. A child cannot live on premises where liquor is sold. Not in my precinct."

In the kitchen Tulip finally succumbs to the violence of her stomach cramps.

"I'm sick," she cries out.

Someone scoops her up; someone else runs to find Myrna. Diarrhea no longer waits, like God, in the wings.

In front Captain Kolevitch wobbles to his feet and searches for the headwaiter. Questioning is imminent.

"Kolevitch," Lew calls out, "I swear I have never done anything illegal in my entire life except maybe adultery. Wrong, yes. Illegal, no! NOBODY LIVES HERE. THIS IS A RESTAURANT."

Myrna, in her finest role, wearing a borrowed Persian lamb coat, strolls past, hiding a gray-faced Tulip under the fur. It is as close to being pregnant as she has been able to manage in her young life. She revolves through the door. Outside she grabs Tulip by the hand and races for her apartment and the bathroom.

Kolevitch finally corners Misha.

Terrified of Cossacks, Misha tells everything.

Lew Krale still remembers Christmas coming that year in New York blessing everything with snow; remembers the immense snowy sadness hanging over the entire world, able to think of nothing but finding Tulip, and of her mother in Mt. Sinai Hospital. He took to walking the cold streets flirting with his old friend, failure, in its most extreme forms—death by walking in December without an overcoat, death by not looking both ways when crossing 53rd Street. One midnight, in a parking lot on Broadway, he howled to the sky, "Bring her back, God, Myrna, whoever. Don't do this." Nobody noticed.

As a gesture of hope or exhaustion he left up the Christmas decorations, the gold streamers and the red balls surrounding the lights in the dining room. I'll take them down when Tulip is back, he thought.

The long drought was over at the RR; apparently the change was permanent. First lunches, now dinners were up—and stayed up. The same new fancy media types Kolevitch had anatomized in his merciless way were there to stay. And Lew was denied even the pleasures of his long romance with failure. He didn't need the acerbic style of Krasner to tell him it had all been bullshit, a pose, a parody of his Russian-Jewish grandparents. His muttered What does it all mean? had lost all conviction because it was no longer rhetorical. Now he wanted an answer!

None came. The small band of regulars who had drifted away returned. From New Year's Eve on they took turns, as if the restaurant was a place of mourning, arriving shortly before closing time: Clurman after writing a theater review, Balanchine after a performance at the City Center; actors who would have gone to Sardi's for a drink and home to bed sat up, instead with Lew . . . the comedians who had gone on to better things came back for the bad times . . . Krasner returned to the scene of his crime and told and retold Operation Tulip . . . the musicians just back from a tour came for hot tea with preserves in the Russian style . . . even Paul Buchalter suspended hostilities to sit silently at the mourner's table . . . Joe Larrabie came with medical bulletins: Katherine Eudemie's life was dwindling down in a room at the Guggenheim Pavillion which Jackson Eudemie could not afford.

All through the beginning of the new year they rerehearsed the scene when Kolevitch had come back with a search warrant and two other cops the day after his lunch with Lew. They'd searched. They'd sought

out Lew who no longer had to lie in the awful absence
of Tulip and Myrna. The next target was the headwaiter,
since Misha had spilled everything the day before.

The only problem was Morris was on duty, not his
brother. Snotty, sardonic Morris, afraid of nothing and
fanatically protective of Lew.

"I never told you anything."

"Don't lie to an officer of the law."

"I never saw you before."

"You're under arrest."

"I'll sue you blind."

Kolevitch took Lew aside. "Look," he said. "I don't
want to arrest anybody. We just don't want a kid shack-
ing up in a restaurant in this precinct."

"She's not. Even if she was before, which she wasn't."

"But your headwaiter confessed it all, yesterday. And
now he's lying."

"He's not."

"My eyes are not crazy."

Krasner descends, slowly, from his cashier's perch
and makes his way through the customers waiting to
be seated, those holding numbered checks trying to
redeem belongings from a bewildered Sasha and those
simply milling around in the excitement of a bust at
the RR. Krasner has been in a moody state since the
vanishing act. Some think he feels implicated as the
author of Operation Tulip; some think he feels bereft
but, being Krasner, can not express his feelings about
the loss of Tulip because he has no text for it. Everyone
watches Krasner take center stage.

He raises his hand; a gaunt messenger in one of the
Shakespeare Histories. In seconds the place is hushed.
Krasner speaks—rather he sings out—his words ringing
with conviction.

"Who prosecutes innocence, persecutes all;
Who nurtures wrong,

Stifles song,
Mocks justice and repeats the Fall."
Lew Krale and Kolevitch turn towards him, silent mouths open.
"Let no one speak for the child we saw
But caring Mother,
Significant Other,
And least of all, false-caring Law."
Several people holding coats sit down at the nearest booths even if occupied by equally startled customers in the middle of their lunch. Morris whispers to Lew, "What play is that from?"
"Ssshhh."
"We serve this world by marrying danger:
Here the child was saved,
Now safety's waived—
Seek her alive in places stranger."
"Does he know where she is?" Kolevitch murmurs.
"That's not what he said," Lew replies.
"Punishment's not your rightful role;
Rescue's nearer the heart and soul.
To love and take is only human.
The secret lies with tormented woman."
"Oh, my God," Kolevitch says, "It's another frustrated-mother babysnatching."
In the turmoil that follows, Kolevitch and his cops rush out to start a kidnapping alert. Tall, central, calm, an eye in a storm, Krasner greets the man in the Chesterfield coat and homburg who hands him his card.
"You are very good," Kermit Bloomgarden says. "I'm casting *Henry the Fourth* . . ."
"Pirandello or Shakespeare?" Krasner asked.
". . . Part 1. You have a big style. You're going to have a big career." The producer smiled. "If you don't call me, I'll call you. At least I know where to find you—for now." Krasner is beyond irony for the moment.

As if sleepwalking, he recites, "I'll address your business, my good Lord, hard upon the hour."

"My good Lord," Sasha breathes. Krasner has finally done an audition!

Applause rolls from table to table, led by Pierre and the other waiters, who have long since given up on Krasner's acting career. Bloomgarden makes his exit and Lew thinks mournfully that if his mother was still alive she would come in and handle the cash register until he finds a new cashier.

Krasner bows, dripping sweat, eyes bulging, catatonic; a star!

The disappearance of Myrna and Tulip spoke to everyone differently. It roused Kolevitch to rage; it spoke poignantly as an absence to the many customers who'd grown used to seeing Tulip's playful education in progress. And it gave Lew a sense of despair so awful, he stopped drinking. As usual, Kolevitch was wrong even though he was right. On arrival at the Eudemie home he was told that Tulip was visiting grandparents in Vancouver. Thus there was no missing child and no one except RR regulars would notice Myrna's extra-long absence from the front.

Furious, Kolevitch questioned everyone! He asked Balanchine about Russian lessons, Blatas about dancing instruction, and Yevshenkowitz about French studies. Ionesco had already left town. The cop questioned Misha and Morris three times, though it's not certain that he ever knew he was embroiled in a twin trompe l'oeil. Katherine Eudemie was often in the hospital when he came to call and Jackson's story was steadfast: his daughter had grown to be the pet of the RR, nothing more. Such things happened in these circles.

Kolevitch would have loved to demand to see the child. But his nerve always collapsed. He was, after all, a failed artist, not an achieved one—thus he was afraid to appear foolish in public. After some mutterings about summonses and subpoenas he subsided. Saroyan would have persisted—would have made a grand drama. The captain made brief comedy; Opera Buffa.

And what of the Opera Seria—Myrna and Tulip's flight? No one has the full story. Some late tellings of furnished rooms, of temporary waitress jobs and lots of Rooms at the Inn; of midnight sweats, of panicked phone calls and last minute hang-ups, of anxiety attacks re scarlet fever or mumps—which turn out to be only a transitory rash or a day's swelling—at these we can only guess.

Pretty good guesses!

What do we know?

First, the RR: we know that the front was now a Place of Desolation! Sans Tulip, sans Myrna. And sans Krasner who was up to his cool snout in *Henry The Fourth Part 1*. The back was a Place Of Exaltation. The Operation Tulip boom was apparently permanent. But full tables could not console Lew. He devoted himself to helping Jackson Eudemie pay for Katherine's expensive illness. And to the activities of several private investigators, who turned up no leads. Katherine grew thinner and Tulip remained invisible.

Until one day winter broke into spring. Fifty-Seventh Street bloomed, plastered with posters of visiting Midwest Symphony Orchestras and the spring crop of recently escaped Russian and Czech violinists, pianists, and cellists. New York in the spring grants freedom to everyone.

On April second, on the eighteenth floor of New York Hospital, Myrna appeared. She tried to bring Tulip up with her but the uniformed security guard said no dice and Myrna had to go up alone. The whole floor smelled overripe, sick-sweet, like spring gone wrong. Listen, spring goes wrong sometimes.

"Hello, Mrs. Eudemie . . ."
"Yes? Who?"
"It's me. I'm Myrna Morris."
"Who?"
"Myrna. From the Russian Rendezvous. Please don't yell. There's no need to call for anybody . . ."
"Oh . . ."
"Tulip's downstairs. They said children are a problem on hospital floors."
". . . I wasn't going to yell. I don't have the strength. I'm glad to see you, Myrna. Is my baby all right?"
"She's terrific. We're reading *Treasure Island*."
"I knew it. It's stupid and absurd but I knew it. Jackson wanted to call the police, but I made him admit that we were as much children as Tulip. We never really took charge of her—all screwed up we are. I supposed desperate people shouldn't have children but everybody has children . . . and you took charge I told him . . . you were not the desperate one . . . you were up to the responsibility. I knew from the way you were in the restaurant how grown-up you were with Tulip— a born mother—I'm rattling on—it's not just Tulip coming back, though I'm thrilled—it's the medicine . . . they're giving me some kind of cortisone—and it makes you speed . . . an experimental program . . . they can't cure me but I'm supposed to cure the rest of the human race, which is okay with me, though it gives me nosebleeds they can't stop . . . I'm speeding but I'm so glad to see you standing here by my bed with Tulip downstairs where she belongs . . . what made you decide to

come back no it doesn't matter please sit down Myrna
. . ." And for a few moments Katherine speeds toward
making some sense of her life, sad but still sense. She
tells Myrna of her mismated childhood heroes, Scott
Fitzgerald and Saul Bellow, Willa Cather and Lionel
Trilling—an innocent from the dry Midwest enchanted
with sea-dreams of the East—how she, Katherine Eudemie, came East for all her firsts: first book, first ocean,
first love, first big splash—and then drowned in the
long, receding wave of reputation.

Myrna sits, stoned with unwanted information. It has
taken all her energy to get to the hospital and she only
vaguely knows who these writers are. She expected
rage, threats, anything but a literary memoir of regret.
She is impatient.

Katherine slows down. "What I remember most is
Fitzgerald's saying he was a poor caretaker of his talent.
Me too. Poor caretaker of everything."

Myrna cannot take any more. "Listen," she says. "I
never really had time to read after I finished school.
Just plays. Maybe that's why I thought it was so amazing
that it was a writer who was leaving me her child—
but I don't feel educated or qualified to talk or even
listen about Fitzgerald and those. But I did love taking
care of Tulip. It got out of hand. All of a sudden I felt
as if she was my only chance. I didn't have a part for
a year-and-a-half. Nothing! Not even an Equity Library
Showcase. Zero! Then Tulip came along. I never understood why. But there she was. I had to tell her a lie
when I ran away, that her mother was sick and her
father couldn't take care of her and that I'd been chosen
to take care of her . . ."

"You were right."

"No, I was crazy. But I want to thank you, Mrs.
Eudemie."

"We have the same child; I think you can call me Katherine."

Myrna stumbled on the words, "Katherine—Kath—Katherine," she said. "It's stupid to thank somebody when you take something from them—but thanks."

Katherine then, turning for some reason to lie on her side, speaks to Myrna sitting behind her, passionately, with all the desperate concern for being understood that a patient brings to the discourse of analysis, at certain moments. "I worked and worked on my new career. I knew how sick I was—so I've had a very short career as a lay analyst—about a year. And I've really had one patient: myself. One patient and one major symptom—if you think symptoms are the name of the game and I don't. In spite of that I've been working on the parapraxes—the slips, forgetting Tulip over and over again—but especially the beginning when it was still a single slip—before you and the others got involved . . . and all I could come up with was the old explanations, chewed-over modernist bullshit—the creative spirit turns destructive when it's blocked . . . that I was sacrificing my only successful creation in revenge for screwing up as a writer. Oh, none of it matters except that you were right, Myrna."

Katherine Eudemie turns back and scares the hell out of Myrna by grabbing her and hugging the young woman to her. She cries out, "You were right, you were chosen to take care of her . . . take her back . . . take her back . . . go downstairs, take her back and finish reading *Treasure Island*. I trust you . . ." But while she is telling her to go she is holding on tightly and all Myrna can think of is she has finally gotten her marbles back and brought the kid to her mother who is losing hers.

To make it worse Katherine Eudemie's nose starts to bleed. This makes for a shocking sight when Jackson Eudemie walks in. He has come to the hospital to visit his wife and found his missing daughter reading a book by Robert Louis Stevenson in the lobby and excitedly brought her up to the room over the protests of Security. There is blood all over the sheets and the women are holding each other as if in a death-struggle. Jackson Eudemie plunges to the bed even though he is still holding Tulip.

Myrna was crying out to all of them—and to the nurses who finally heard the uproar and came flying in—"Don't you want to know why I brought the kid back? All you care about is your own goddamn selves not about her." They froze in some hideous red-speckled, white-sheeted version of Laocöon's struggle. "I sent her to the store to get some cartons of milk and cereal, stuff like that, and she got all giant sizes and she was wobbling up the stairs, a walk-up in Dover, New Jersey, and when she saw me she said, 'Myrna, help, help, Myrna.' And I grabbed the stuff from her and I almost stopped breathing because I got it, I got so clearly that it was over. She never asked for anything before and now I knew we were in trouble and I knew it was over . . ."

But by this time the nurses who represented the Official World of Help had taken over and the Opera Seria was finished.

Finally it doesn't matter how you got where you are. It matters where you are and where you're going. Katherine went to sleep at last two days later. Tulip, having been away from home so long under the cover story of being with her grandparents in Vancouver, actually went to Canada immediately. Finding themselves alone, Myrna and Jackson Eudemie inevitably found each other.

Eleven months later they were married and Tulip came home.

Myrna and Jackson already had little lovers' tricks of word play. One of them was this: he would say, "Everything begins in lust," and she would reply, as they dozed off, "Everything ends in sleep." Or she'd say, "Everything begins in curiosity," and he'd say, "Everything ends in boredom." It was part of his attempt at a literary corruption of Myrna.

Before they decided to get married, Jackson accused her of going through with it just to get Tulip after all. What he said was: "Everything begins in planning." And her denial was: "Everything ends in luck."

"I heard you were in love with Lew Krale."

"That was more of my own craziness. It would have been nice."

"It would have been awful. Do you know Lew?"

"He used to ask my advice. I liked that. But it seems to me I was really in love with Katherine."

"Oh"

"She came to see me and we walked in the park. Everything about her—even her troubles—dumping a baby day after day—it all seemed glamorous. I was taking part in a fairy tale. I read her book. I loved that she was a writer."

"Romanticism. You ended up with the editor."

She laughed. "And the child."

It had never occurred to Jackson Eudemie that he would marry again after Katherine died. But that was about

as unoriginal as most of his ideas. And if Myrna did
marry him for his child it didn't quite work since
boarding school, college, and Tulip's own marriage came
it seemed in a matter of minutes. Myrna had been
prescient about her childless destiny. She could not
conceive. Tulip *had* been her last chance. What Myrna
got was Jackson Eudemie and a small press the two of
them operate now, twenty-two years later, from their
house in Greenwich, Connecticut.

And what of Tulip? What was she thinking and feeling
during all that tumult of attention, of education of
abduction, of being jolted, pulled, and pushed to be this
or that emblem for the adults in the RR universe. It's
interesting to speculate and observe because only a few
weeks ago, more than two decades after these events,
a reporter for *Time* magazine heard the story at the RR.
The intellectual Lindbergh case with a happy ending
was how he sold the story to his editors and he cornered
the grown-up Tulip, now twenty-four years old and a
publicist for the Mark Taper Forum and married to a
tax lawyer, Reuben Rosenfeld, who also collected first
folio Shakespeare.

"Oh, yes," Tulip said. "I remember it all. My mother
was agitated and wild, a poet after all. I don't think I
knew then what I'm saying now but I knew, somehow!
My father, he was something else again: elegant, eloquent, great style, and full of love. He could have been
a great man in publishing but he wouldn't make the
necessary compromises." (Jackson Eudemie would have
been astonished at such notions. He knew he was only
a Hack playing Man of Letters. A harmless game, neither
noble nor ignoble. Children are strange: you get either
hero-worship or rage both usually unfounded in real
cause.)

"But do you recall how you actually felt? The experience of it? Being raised in the hat check room of a restaurant?"

Tulip Rosenfeld thought a moment. "I was only four," she said. "I would have liked to have friends. Once a little girl was allowed to stay with me while her parents had tea on a snowbound day, a real blizzard. We sneaked out and threw snowballs at the box office of Carnegie Hall. Her name was Leslie and she had an eye which drifted."

"Wouldn't that be a screen memory? Not something a four-year-old would notice and remember?"

"Maybe."

"And how could you tell the twin headwaiters from each other when no one else could?"

"It's a knack. Like recognizing shades of color. You just know."

"Weren't you ever frightened?"

"Sometimes I'd be a little triste and long for my mother."

"You have some French words. Didn't you study French at the RR with Ionesco?"

"Short? Bald? Drank a lot?"

"Yes."

"That was the one. Listen, this may not be the best time to interview me about this."

"Why not?"

"I'm pregnant. You get big mood swings when you're going to have a baby."

"Ah . . ."

So—here is Tulip, pregnant! Myrna and Jackson call her immediately. Yes, it is true, she says, Reuben and she had been planning to call them with the news.

Tulip is as cool and steady as her mother was warm and volatile.

"Everything begins in rumors and ends in babies," Myrna jokes.

"Everything begins in *Time* magazine and ends in reality," Jackson Eudemie replies.

At the cemetery Katherine was waiting. What else was there for her to do?

"Katherine," Jackson said, standing at the foot of her grave. "This is hard to believe, but Tulip is having a baby."

"God, Jackson, you're so self-conscious. You could have told me at home."

"It seemed more appropriate here."

"You were always so damned appropriate."

"Listen, I didn't come out to this God-forsaken part of Long Island to have a post-marital argument. I just wanted to tell you you're going to be a grandmother."

"That's neat."

"Grandmother's don't use words like 'neat.' "

"This one does. If I can still can be one—or anything. It's not clear you know."

"I know. I guess."

"How come you never came here before?"

He was silent.

"Is Tulip happy? It's so hard for me to imagine her grown up. And a mother."

"It's hard for me too," Jackson said. "Living doesn't solve anything, you know."

"Neither does dying," Katherine said. "I wish I could go for some therapy and I wish I could finish my novel."

"Me too," Jackson said. "I'm writing fiction, now. After you died I got tired of compiling anthologies.

Myrna thought I should be a real writer. I started a novel. I haven't finished it yet. That was twenty-two years ago."

"Novels are hard," Katherine said.

"I know. I'm back to my old bread and butter. Right now I have an assignment to do a children's version of Freud's *Psychopathology of Everyday Life*. The research is fascinating."

"My God!"

"I have to make a living."

"Of course. Tell Tulip I'm proud my baby's having a baby."

"You know I can't do that," he said.

"I guess not," Katherine said.

It was chilly and the trek back from the cemetery made Jackson hungry. He went back via Manhattan and found himself at the Russian Rendezvous. It was six o'clock, Thursday evening, fall in New York. All of those things. Standing on the sidewalk in front of the RR, Jackson Eudemie shivered and loved them all passionately at that moment: twilight, midweek, autumn, midtown New York; loved them as you can only love such things right after a visit to the cemetery. He faced East and it was as if the long line of "civilians"—that's what Lew Krale used to call ordinary people with no claim to an art form, whose names would never appear in either *The Hudson Review* or *Variety*—it was as if they were all heading up the slight slope of Fifty-seventh Street, all the way from the East River, toward a dinner at The Russian Rendezvous. He saw them all as "going-to-bes" in that twilight hallucination. After all everyone is en route to something. He was en route to becoming a grandfather and had just come from a conversation in a cemetery. Everyone is hungry for something if only dinner.

Jackson sat in a front booth and ordered a giant meal: zakuska—spicy Russian hors d'oeuvres, borscht, hot in honor of the first cool fall evening, karsky shashlik, and tea. By the time he finished, the pre-concert crowd was thick in the front waiting for tables, his included. But when he went to pay the check Jackson found that his wallet had not made it back with him from the graveyards of Long Island.

How embarrassing! He had not seen Lew Krale for a couple of years. Lew was gray and gaunt but with a tranquil air, no longer so frantic. He sipped a Seven-up and grinned.

"I see you haven't changed, Jackson," he said. "You still can't pay."

"I see you have changed," Jackson said. He waved at the crowd. "You're drinking Seven-up and I'm the only one who can't pay. I'll send you a check tomorrow."

"Don't sweat it," he said. "I'm up to my ass in checks. Somebody offered to buy me out the other day for three million dollars. I gave him a drink instead."

Jackson told Lew about Tulip getting pregnant and Lew bought them both vodkas. They toasted the impending grandchild.

"Is this okay?" Jackson asked, "you drinking again?"

"I can take it or leave it. Since Tulip. That kid changed everything."

Jackson asked him how it felt to be such a grand success. Lew's face went dark.

"Don't make fun of an old friend."

Jackson swore he'd meant it kindly.

"It doesn't feel right," Lew said. "It feels good—but

not right. You can't change at my age. How about you and Myrna?"

"We're always just getting by. I almost had a best-seller: a book on Great Teas of the World. But it fizzled out. I'm the only publisher in the world who would try to make a coffee table book out of tea. I'm too old to change."

"Listen," Lew Krale said. "Just not dying young is a kind of success."

"It's a kind of failure, too."

His eyes opened wide: the old Lew. "You think so?" he said, a hint of hope in the question.

On the strength of that question the two of them drank the evening to its end. Jackson called Myrna twice with a revised schedule. The headwaiter changed tables around them three times. At last they began to be a problem. Too noisy, old jokes and memories too raucous, and they ended up climbing over the ledge of the hat check room.

"It's okay," Lew muttered to the astonished young woman attendant, "This man's kid used to live here." From the inside looking out they surveyed the debris of their lives. The coat room was three times the size it had been in the Grand Old Period. Lew lay down on the floor, embedded in some of the light topcoats of the season, remembering, aloud, Krasner's moment of dramatic intervention, Tulip's momentous diarrhea.

Drunk and sad, Jackson Eudemie lay down next to Lew. The events of the day made him think of his children's book on Freud, which was, as usual, late. It was a small jump from Lew's mumbled memories to thinking about Freud—the Freud of 1887, turning from the bizarre and terrifying discoveries of hysterical, often paralyzed women delivering up the dark twisted truths they'd spent their lives, their balance, their physical health trying to suppress. He thought of that self-named conquistadore turning from this exotic jungle to the still unexplored jungle of the every day: the tongue slipping into the repressed expressed wish . . . the umbrella forgotten on a rainy day summing up a life of denial . . .

The Psychopathology of Everyday Life! In his silly little children's book he would describe to the young people of the world how the ambitiousness of the title went unnoticed in its familiarity. He thought of Lew Krale drinking himself out of business saved by Tulip, growing old crucified by success; of Krasner lurking in the forest of his shyness and ego, a hero waiting to happen to his own drama. All of these and most of all of his first wife, Katherine Eudemie. She'd come to New York to be a writer like Lionel Trilling, Delmore Schwartz, Bernard Malamud—the great shadow-Jews of her Midwest imagination. She'd come to contribute and willy-nilly she will have contributed.

She'd come to New York for grandeur and forgot what she came for. Parapraxis Found was her most lasting work and she'd ended up helping to save Lew Krale's dying restaurant . . . had written, instead of the Great Jewish/Goyish Novel, a chapter in the history of a café; the Necessary Place, where those with a song to sing rest their voices in gossip and laughter. It was the dream of artistic achievement writ small, not in ink but in caviar and canapés.

Thus go most dreams when they encounter the Psychopathology of Everyday Life. Remembering all this he began to laugh not unkindly and Lew joined in with a loose, wet laugh, creating the kind of ruckus the place had not heard or seen in years.

"How'd you get home?" Myrna said.

"Lew lent me some money. It was like the old days. Go to sleep."

But before they slept he told her about the crazy evening. He left out the cemetery part; told her everything else, though, including the drunken sprawl with Lew Krale in the hat check room. He felt old and happy and unreasonably pleased with the past.

"I hope Tulip appreciates being pregnant," Myrna said. "I wanted that so much."

"Yes. Everything begins in passion and hunger," Jackson Eudemie said.

"I was never a mother and now I'm going to be a grandmother," Myrna murmured. "Everything ends in comedy," she said and went back to sleep.